ROSIE

After living in an enclosed order for twenty years, Sister Marie Rose is sent to Medjugorje, Yugoslavia, to find out more about the reported miracles taking place there. Events take a quite unexpected turn, though, when she meets Bill and they visit London, and then her native Wales, together . . . A few exciting months later, Rosie's mind is in turmoil — should she obey her Reverend Mother's instruction to return to the convent? Married to Christ, how could she break her vows?

MARK CARTER
co-writer:
JOAN STANLEY

ROSIE

Complete and Unabridged

ULVERSCROFT
Leicester

First published in Great Britain in 2006 by
Red'n'Ritten Ltd.
Steyning

First Large Print Edition
published 2007
by arrangement with
Red'n'Ritten Ltd.
Steyning

British Library CIP Data

Carter, Mark
    Rosie.—Large print ed.—
    Ulverscroft large print series: general fiction
    1. Nuns—Fiction
    2. Large type books
    I. Title
    823.9'2 [F]

    ISBN 978–1–84617–971–6

1

In the first grey light she was close to the big concrete cross, which the villagers had put up more than half a century ago. The sky was clear, the air crisp, and far below she could just make out the village church with its twin spires, the little farmhouses and the patchwork fields of maize and tobacco. Everything was still in that moment before sunrise when the whole world seems to hold its breath.

It was easier to think up here. Easier to try and make some sense of the way in which she had been catapulted into the outside world.

*   *   *

For twenty years she had been enclosed in the Abbey, never allowed outside the main gates. And during all that time she had never read a newspaper, listened to a radio or watched a television set.

The Reverend Mother was the only person to possess a radio. She avidly followed the news from Medjugorje, where, on a hilltop close to the village, six young children had witnessed the appearance of the Virgin Mary.

Many times they had received messages and, consequently, people from all over the world were making pilgrimages to this place.

In accordance with a certain modernisation and the relaxation of discipline in the religious houses, the Reverend Mother decided to send one of her sisters. She would go as a representative of the ancient Abbey of St. John's, and report back on the extraordinary events, which seemed to be taking place there. Having gained the consent of the Bishop the nuns drew lots, and Sister Mary Rose was the lucky winner.

There would be no preparation, not even a visit to the local town, Rockensand: the Reverend Mother believed the best way to learn to swim was to jump in at the deep end. After all, God would always be present.

Sister Mary Rose was told to wear civilian clothes for the journey, so nobody in the wicked world outside would stare at her. She climbed into the convent attic: that same gloomy place where, all those years ago, at the age of eighteen, her suitcase had been stored.

Most of the moth-eaten items fell apart. She remembered dimly that she had put her 'best outfit' away in a big plastic bag in the bottom of the case. The clothes inside, although musty smelling, remained in a good condition: a brown tweed skirt, a couple of pullovers, and — she caught her breath — the old, red anorak she had worn as a teenager for hiking. She found some old coins in one of the pockets: two half-crowns, a couple of shillings and several pennies. The first money she had touched in all that time. And a letter from her boyfriend, Bob, imploring her not to leave him. He would be over forty, married, probably, with children.

Rummaging through the suitcase she found some completely forgotten, personal things. She picked up an old black and white photograph: a lovely girl with fair hair and summer in her eyes looked back at her. She felt a sudden dread, and tipping everything out of the suitcase she searched for a mirror. The smell of cheap perfume, bought so long ago, brought back such haunting memories.

Her handbag! A small mirror fell out. She snatched it up. But all she could see in the dim light was a pale, ghostly face.

What was she was doing? Breaking her vows, disobeying God, being utterly vain. She stuffed everything back into the suitcase; everything except the brown tweed skirt, one of the pullovers and her old friend the red anorak.

The Reverend Mother gave her a lecture on how she should conduct herself in the outside world. She would be away for two weeks and whenever possible she would keep the same discipline and conduct herself as if she were still in the convent. She would pray seven times a day, go to Mass on Sundays and speak to no one unless spoken to. She was to write a comprehensive account of what was happening in Medjugorje, and she would be expected to give a lecture on the subject when she returned.

Her departure was timed to coincide with mid-morning prayers, so that nobody would see her leaving the Abbey in civilian clothes. Although the clothes fitted well and the skirt was quite long she felt distinctly uncomfortable after wearing a loose-fitting robe for all those years. What if everybody stared at her when she stepped outside?

Everything had been arranged for her: the hired car to the airport, the plane tickets and modest accommodation in a Medjugorje farmhouse. She was given a little money and she spent some time working out the currency, both the English and Yugoslav.

★   ★   ★

So many people! Pale, taut faces. Smiling faces. Cruel faces. Strange and sometimes dreadful-looking clothes. The drive to the airport scared her enough; it must have been

4

twenty years since she had travelled in a motorcar. Inside, she was pushed and shoved about until she became quite disorientated.

'Calm yourself, Sister Mary Rose!' What would the Reverend Mother think of her? She was already in a spin, and she had not left the country yet. Sister Mary Rose! How could she be expected to cope on her own? It was so long since she had been out in the world by herself. She would have been quite capable of taking herself to the Abbey on her own at eighteen years of age! Look at all the young people dashing about, how self-assured they are.

She had plenty of time before take off. She would just sit quietly and collect herself. She would have liked to call her mother, who lived alone in a cottage in Wales, but she couldn't make the telephone work. She longed to hear the no-nonsense voice. Somehow, she must see her before returning to the Abbey. True, her mother had visited her last Christmas. She usually managed to come about once a year, but the journey was more than she could afford.

She remembered how her mother had accompanied her to the Abbey on that glorious summer's day twenty years ago. All the talking over. Her parents had done their best to persuade her to continue her studies for an agricultural degree. They had known that given time, and a chance to see something of the world, she would grow out of it. But her early churchgoing years, her study of the Bible that she had read from cover to cover, and the school nativity plays in which she invariably wanted to play the part of Mary, had imbued her with more than an ordinary desire to come closer to God. She had been determined to take her vows.

A few years later her father had died. Soon after her brother had been killed in a car crash. How could a loving God be so cruel? Was her rightful place alongside her grieving mother? Should she leave the Abbey? After all, wouldn't that be serving God better? She had confessed all this to the Reverend Mother only to be reminded that she had made her vows: she had become a Bride of Christ and nothing on earth could undo that. Penance had duly been done.

'Would the passengers travelling to Dubrovnik please proceed to . . . '

She stood up suddenly. 'Oh, I didn't hear what she said! What am I to do?'

Some kind person took her arm and helped her into the departure lounge, and eventually she boarded the aircraft to Yugoslavia.

The huge jet roared down the runway.

Such vibration! Surely this massive contraption must fall to bits. And then it took off, sweeping her to the sky; she was terrified. Other passengers hid their fear in drink. Apart from communion wine, she had never tasted alcohol in her life, and could only sit there and wonder how on earth such a monster-plane could ever come down to earth safely.

★ ★ ★

From Dubrovnik she took the ninety-mile coach journey to Medjugorje, and found her lodgings without much difficulty. After a couple of lazy days, torch in hand, she set out while it was still dark to climb Mount Krizivac. It seemed everybody who went to Medjugorje scaled the mountain, or tried to.

The stiff walk up the boulder-strewn track was exhausting. Past all the empty tins, old newspapers and litter left by the tourists. Past the Stations Of The Cross until, at last, she reached the summit and the mountain, she felt, belonged to her.

She stared at the big concrete cross and wondered how many men it would have taken to haul it up to the top of the mountain. Her eyes wandered over the panorama and its breath-taking beauty. The church of St. James down in the valley was huge for the size of the village. Church! It would soon be time to go. Mass would be at ten o'clock. Just a few more minutes. She would watch the sunrise and then she would have to find her way back down the mountainside and take the long walk to the village.

★   ★   ★

The authorities at the large seminary in Yugoslavia issued a general invitation to other members of their order to come to Medjugorje and see for themselves what was happening. Surprisingly, when the Abbot of St. Joseph's called for volunteers, only one man stepped forward: William Oldham, or Brother Bill to a few close friends. Brother Bill had only been in the monastery for ten years. All the others had lived and worked there, perched high above the sea on a remote Hebridean rock called Toy, for much longer. The general feeling was that an excursion into the world outside was to be avoided at all costs, even if it was to Medjugorje. And because the Vatican had failed to issue a ruling on the matter nobody at St. Joseph's really believed the Virgin Mary could be seen there.

A well-built man, Bill Oldham looked more

8

like a prize fighter than a monk. Once, his boat had capsized in heavy seas; he had escaped with his life, but his nose had been broken. This had given him a somewhat battered appearance, as if the storms that struck the rock had weathered him, too. He was not a handsome man. But so genial was his manner that people smiled as he approached.

For Bill, life in the monastery had become distinctly monotonous. And for some time he had been asking himself, 'Is it really necessary to be shut away from society in order to contemplate God?'

The same answer dogged him: he would probably feel closer to God if he were to join in with the hurly-burly of the world outside; where life could be seen and experienced in all its goodness and depravity. This trip to Yugoslavia would be a welcome break from the monastery.

For his part, the old Abbot was pleased when Brother Bill volunteered to go; he had been a disturbing influence lately and it would be good to acknowledge the invitation. The reproachful looks on the brother's faces reflected their thoughts: to leave the island would be to dwell among sinners, and the old Abbot would never have allowed anybody to leave the monastery if he had not received an express invitation from his contemporaries overseas.

The monks of St. Joseph's were allowed to pursue their various interests. Brother Bill's particular hobby was photography. Over the years he had taken so many pictures of the monastery, the sunsets and his fellow monks that many of his shots were practically identical. He was being offered two weeks in which to photograph the world! Yugoslavia, at least! The outside world would be a photographer's dream.

And, who knows, two weeks might be enough out there. If he could bring back all the photographs he had ever wished for, he might stay on in the monastery after all. And then he would not have to suffer the humiliation of resigning in front of the Abbot and all the others.

★   ★   ★

Brother Bill had found lodging in one of the small homesteads close to the church in Medjugorje. After a good night's sleep, his first desire was to climb Mount Krizivac, from the top of which he would capture the spectacle of the sun coming up from the horizon. He rose early, packed a flask of coffee, and set off. It was good to be back in civilian clothes, to blend in, no longer a source of whispered comment.

The climb was steep. He was fitter than he thought. He was not the least bit exhausted. The chill air in those last minutes before dawn was positively invigorating. He stretched out his arms to embrace the world and in praise of his God Who had created the wonders spread out before him. But he was not alone. A woman stood in the thin mist that wreathed the mountain.

As the sun came up he saw that she was fair, not dark like Mary. He wanted to photograph the early sun in all its glory. What he did not want was anybody in the way, spoiling the view. Hang it all, if you can't get away from people at five o'clock in the morning on top of a mountain in Yugoslavia, where can you go! He could not very well tell her to move on and, when he took the picture, there she was — right in the middle of it. He moved up close to her, but she did not move.

Mid-thirties? He noticed how the early sun brought out the natural highlights in her hair. And there was a peace in her eyes. She had that certain something, which a painter would strive to portray. She smiled, 'It's going to be a wonderful day!' She had a pretty voice, too. English or Welsh, if he was not mistaken.

Brother Bill forgot about the sunrise, and somehow he didn't mind her being up there after all. He got his pictures and if there happened to be a pretty woman in the middle of one of them, well, it would make them all sit up when he passed them round at the monastery! She was about to start off down the track, but he stopped her. 'Have you been out here long?'

Was she nervous of him? He had spoken to several people on his way out to Yugoslavia and had never provoked this reaction. He did not like to think of himself as conceited, but he was aware that most people responded to his natural laid-back charm. And she seemed to be such a gentle soul . . . It was as though she was debating with herself whether she should continue the conversation or not. Then she visibly relaxed, 'I only arrived two days ago.'

'Are you on holiday?'

'No, not really. I came out here on a fact-finding job.'

'What, about Medjugorje? The visionaries?'

'Yes.'

She was a schoolteacher, no doubt, or a writer. Some of them he remembered could be shy, retiring people. He hesitated to enquire about her work; he did not want to frighten her back into her shell.

'You look as if you could do with some hot coffee.' Maybe it was because he had not spoken to a woman for years, but he did not want her to go. He did not want to tell her he was a monk, either — she would probably run a mile. He took out his flask and poured some coffee. 'Here, this'll set you up!'

He remembered, too late, that he had added some whisky to the flask and he hoped it would not be too strong for her.

★　★　★

She couldn't remember having coffee before, certainly not at the Abbey. All they ever had there had been wishy-washy tea. This tasted good and it seemed to put new life into her. She drank it down quickly. She should be going; she wanted to get back in time for Mass. And she was beginning to feel uncomfortably hot in her thick tweed skirt and anorak.

He was obviously beginning to feel the first heat of the sun, too; he took off his jacket and started to unbutton his shirt, as if it were the most natural thing to do. Sister Mary Rose could not remember seeing a bare-chested man, except her father in the garden long ago. But what about the time when one of the men who was mending the roof of the Abbey

13

took his shirt off? The Reverend Mother very quickly appeared on the scene and told him to put it back on again!

The only thing that stopped Sister Mary Rose from making her excuses and hurrying away there and then was the large cross this man wore round his neck. Had she not read somewhere that sailors sometimes wore crosses. He was very tanned and rugged-looking. That was it! He was probably a sailor. And surely anybody who wore a cross like that would be completely harmless. She fingered the slightly rusty zip of her anorak. Why did it have to stick, now?

'Hey, the sun's quite hot already. Why don't you take that thing off?'

Take her anorak off in front of him! She was only wearing a light cotton blouse. In her mind's eye, a frowning Reverend Mother was standing right in front of her. She would unzip the anorak a little. 'The sun is not that high. It must be the coffee.'

She gave the zip a tug, but it did not move. She tugged both ways; it refused to budge.

'Here, let me have a go.'

Startled, she took a step back and nearly fell over. 'Please. I am all right. I will keep it on for the walk down. It will still be cold on that side of the mountain. I really should be going now, there's a ten o'clock Mass and I shall be late.'

'I've taken all the photos I want for now. Let's go down together.'

2

The path zigzagged down the mountainside with the whole of Yugoslavia, or so it seemed, spread out before them. They climbed down a rocky slope and came to the lane that led across countryside to the village. Bill pointed to the hill where the children had first seen the Virgin Mary. 'Coach loads of people will be climbing all over that hill today.' Unable to contain his curiosity he asked, 'Are you a school teacher or something?' She was a little way ahead of him, and if she heard him she made no reply, and he did not have the courage to ask her again.

There were pilgrims everywhere, and if it hadn't been for the red anorak he would have lost her. The church precincts were beautifully laid out with flowers, shrubs and olive trees. Benches were provided for people who preferred to sit outside the building in the fresh air, and listen to the service from booming loudspeakers. He tried to stay with her, but she was carried into the church by the surge of humanity.

He waited there, and when the service ended and the people flooded out of the church he pushed his way through, searching for her red coat. He caught up with her at last. Did he imagination it, or was that a faint look of reproof, because he had not followed her into the church?

★   ★   ★

While they sat there together she tried to think of some excuse to go back to her lodging, but whatever she said would be a lie, and as far as she could remember she hadn't told a lie for years.

She looked fearfully about her. One of the priests, like some bird of prey, stared at her. Could he tell, in some mysterious way, that she was a nun and that she was consorting with a complete stranger? Back at the Abbey she would have been safe, but those protecting walls were a long way away. In this strange and frightening outside world, there were more things to disturb one's soul than she could have imagined. Love thy neighbour: all that had been taken for granted in the convent at St. John's Abbey. This man she met on the mountaintop, this stranger, was he a neighbour?

'I'm Bill Oldham.'

'Oh!' She took his outstretched hand. 'Sis . . . ' she gulped, 'Er, Rose, Mary Rose.'

'That's a pretty name!'

She could feel the colour rise in her cheeks. Nobody had ever told her that — except perhaps Bob, and he had been out of her life for so long . . . She began to feel guilty. She should have come out with it: explained that she was a nun. He would have moved on politely and that would have been that. But after being shut up in the Abbey for so long she was lonely, and not a little afraid, and this Bill Oldham seemed a friendly sort of man. What was wrong with talking to a fellow countryman in a foreign land? Surely the Reverend Mother would approve?

As if by way of further introduction he continued, 'More than ten million people have been here already, so I came over to see what all the fuss was about.'

'What do you think happened? Do you believe those children really saw the Virgin Mary?'

'Most of these things happen in hot countries where the peasants are more superstitious,' Bill observed. 'You never hear of Mary appearing in, say, Leeds or Bradford. Then again there may be something in self-hypnosis. The children saw something and they wanted to believe it was her. After all, people claim that they can see ghosts.

Imagination can be a very powerful thing!'

Rosie was shocked at his scepticism. 'I believe they saw her. I heard those children were subjected to very rigorous tests, and they underwent physical and psychiatric examinations and were found to be perfectly sane and fit. The authorities were bothered, though, because of the huge crowds, which were being drawn to this place. Being a Communist State, they were worried that the whole thing could develop into political unrest. There have been so many unaccountable things in this world. Take the miracles for instance. Yes, I believe those children did see her. The very first time was on that hill near here in 1981 and they have been seeing her ever since in various other places in the village.'

'And you came over here to write about it?'

'Yes.'

'Well, this place has got all the makings of a good story, and just think of the wonderful pictures you can take.'

'Pictures?'

'The church for instance, that statue over there, the little village. And the scenery is fantastic, especially from the top of that mountain. I've been taking so many pictures already I'll have to start an album just for Medjugorje when I get back.'

She hadn't thought of photographs. Cameras simply didn't exist at St. John's. She remembered the camera she had been given in her youth, a birthday present, in those happy carefree far off days. It was probably still there with the rest of her things at her home in Wales.

'Didn't you bring a camera?' Not very efficient if she was, in fact, a reporter.

'I can buy some postcards here . . . '

'Yes, but if you wanted to reproduce them you would have to get permission. You know, copyright and all that. Listen, photography happens to be my hobby. Why don't you show me what you like and I'll take the pictures for you?'

She hesitated. 'He must think I'm a reporter from one of the newspapers!' What about payment? She had only been given enough money for the barest expenses. She was not used to thinking for herself. Back at the convent all the decisions had been made for her, and in that moment all she wanted was to be back safe and sound behind those protecting walls.

'It won't cost you a penny, besides I will probably have some copies done for myself.' He stood up and brought out his camera.

'Hey, what about a picture of you for a start? Over there in front of that statue!'

She looked at the statue. Have her picture taken next to the Virgin Mary? The Reverend Mother would have something to say about that. And yet, lots of people were being photographed, people who had just come out of church, and when a couple of priests came and had their pictures taken she was sure that there would be no harm in one quick snapshot.

She waited until the priests had moved on and went and stood in front of the beautiful white marble statue, and all the time she tried to keep the sun from hurting her eyes.

'Don't look so worried, Rosie. You don't mind me calling you that, do you?' That made her smile and he took the picture quickly. 'There you go. Two lovely-looking ladies in one picture.'

She didn't like that, and shot him a warning look. Before she could say anything he handed her the camera. 'Here, you take one of me.' He showed her how the camera worked and then he went across to the statue.

'You don't mind me calling you Rosie then?' he grinned.

'Not if you don't mind me calling you Bill!' She stopped, appalled. The man was a complete stranger and the words had slipped out, just as if she had been joking with one of the other sisters at the convent, and they did joke, sometimes, even behind those austere walls.

* * *

Brother Bill didn't mind. He was so pleased to have such a pretty and intelligent woman to talk to, and then a sobering thought occurred to him: if he hadn't volunteered to come out here, he'd have missed all this.

He wanted to enjoy her friendship for the brief time that he was free, but if he obeyed his conscience and told her that he was a monk he would be sure to lose her. She would be very tactful, of course, but a monk? A holy man? A happy, if somewhat shy, woman like this would be sure to make some excuse and leave him.

* * *

Rosie, too, had again been wondering whether to own up to her own profession. He would be very nice about it and he would stumble with his excuses, but a nun? He would be sure to walk out on her! Besides, friendship, surely, was a good thing. Bill Oldham seemed to be a lonely man, and to send him away would not be a Christian thing to do. She reassured herself that any friendship, however brief, in this transitory outside world, was better than none.

Bill broke an awkward silence. 'I've got an idea. I've got some time to fill in over here, so let's work together on this story of yours. I'll take care of the photography and I could also help you with the write-up. After all, two heads are better than one!'

Rosie could only feel relief. She was alone and completely out of her depth in a foreign country and Bill Oldham had offered to help her. Well, she could certainly write a better story with the backup of a camera.

'Together, we could do it in half the time' Bill enthused, 'and then we could go for long walks in this beautiful countryside!'

Long walks! The only walk she had been allowed to take had been in the grounds of St. John's Abbey, and from where she had listened to that strange outside world, the world they had all been praying for. She had taken notice of the motorcars and the melancholy hooting of the trains, and wondered about all those passengers, a host of people who swept past unseen. Who were they? And where were they going? Lost souls, who came out of nothing and who disappeared into nothing?

Sometimes the sound of a party going on in the village would hold her attention. What fun it would be to join in, and sing and dance, too. She would try and blot out these selfish thoughts, but the outside world, the roar of transport, the happy-sounding din, which came from the local pub on a Saturday night, would always be there, just outside those big ornamental gates. She was able to hear that world, but the only thing she had been able to see of it was the increasing monstrosity of its aircraft.

And now, incredibly, she had flown in one of those big planes herself and here she was in Yugoslavia of all places! Surely God had given her a helping hand to see something of his wonderful world? All the same she began to feel uneasy, because everything seemed to be going too well, as if in one moment she was dying of thirst and then she was given too much water. Was the devil tempting her, as he had once tried to tempt Christ? Was Bill Oldham, her newfound friend, in fact, the devil?

'What are you thinking about?'

His eyes were blue grey, smiling at her. No, there was nothing about the devil there. Besides, devils didn't wear crosses, or did they? Well, maybe her own cross would cancel his out and she smiled.

'What's the joke?'

'Oh, nothing. It was just something funny.'

'Well, don't keep it all to yourself.'

She tried to think of something to say. 'It was the heading for our newssheet: 'Bill and Rosie see Virgin Mary in Medjugorje!''

Bill laughed. 'Let's celebrate our new found Partnership-In-Print with some lunch.'

They ate in silence, each finding it difficult to break the age-old monastery rule.

★　★　★

Rosie had been shopping for something cooler to wear, and when Bill saw her again she had changed into a brightly coloured cotton skirt, a blouse, and she wore dark glasses. She could tell that he was pleased and she felt good, too, though it did feel strange after wearing a long black gown for twenty years.

The gown was such a positive item of clothing, concealing everything, from neck to ankles. It was warm in the draughty corridors in winter and cool in summer. The gown, with its ample flow of black cloth, carried prestige. Again, her hand strayed to her forehead. It was difficult to get used to going about with a bare head.

She remembered, when she had changed into that awful tweed skirt, how pale her legs had been. They were still shapely and she hoped that in the hot sun they would soon become a nice shade of brown like everybody else's. Vanity? Yes, but how could she stop the thoughts, which came into her head? She tried to shut them out, but the swing door of her mind just let them all back in again!

They spent the afternoon together, writing, and later they went out and mingled with the crowds on Mount Podbrdo, where the vision had first appeared in 1981. The path was covered with big stones and knife-edged rocks, hot to the touch, yet many people climbed about with bare feet. Rosie and Bill explored the surrounding area and took more photographs; in the evening they made their way to Rosie's place to write up their article.

★   ★   ★

'We must have written several pages already.' Bill started to sort out the sheets of paper covered with their notes. 'How long do you want this story to be?'

'About as much again, I would think.'

'That shouldn't be difficult. At the rate we're going we'll finish it in about four days. What about getting it typed though, I suppose you'll be doing all that back in England?'

She hadn't really thought about that. Back

at the convent they had written all their letters by hand. There was an old typewriter in the office, of course, and she might be able to get the secretary to do the work.

'I can type,' Bill offered. 'I'll have a scout round the village and see if I can borrow a typewriter.'

Again, Bill wondered what she did for a living; surely a reporter would be much better prepared. He didn't know much about journalism, but he was certain that they would be much more experienced and would never write up their reports by hand.

What did it matter as long as she didn't discover what he did! Sooner or later she would ask him about his job and he didn't want to tell her an outright lie. Back on the island he had been responsible for the vegetable garden and tilled a piece of land to grow crops. Yes, that was it; he would tell her that he did a bit of farming.

★   ★   ★

During the next few days they interviewed the local priest, as well as the visionaries and several pilgrims. Many of the pilgrims who flocked to Medjugorje were baffled by the events, which were still taking place there. And though the Vatican had refused to give a positive ruling, the local priest, after many searching questions to the children, concluded that the hand of God was evident and the episodes were genuine. The centre for everything that was happening in Medjugorje was the church of St. James, where powerful preaching that stressed prayer and conversion took place several times a day.

In the main, the messages given by the Virgin Mary referred to the turbulent state of the world, and stressed the only ways to peace and the salvation of souls, were prayer, penance and fasting. This in itself caused debate amongst non Catholic Christians who believe the only way to God is through belief in Jesus, and there is nothing we can do to earn eternal life.

★ ★ ★

'I didn't tell you, Rosie, I have found a typewriter! The local tourist office said I could go there tomorrow and use theirs.'

'That's wonderful, Bill.'

'It'll take me the best part of a day to get it done . . . It means we won't see much of each other tomorrow.'

'You could come and see me later . . . in the evening — maybe . . . ' Rose looked away. She knew in her heart that she was straying well beyond what the Reverend Mother would consider acceptable behaviour for one of her nuns. But she couldn't help herself. She was unlikely to have this kind of freedom to enjoy friendship with anyone outside the Abbey ever again. And with a man at that.

He gave her a boyish smile, 'You just try and stop me! For one thing I shall expect praise and admiration for a report brilliantly presented . . . '

'All right, Bill.' She laughed, 'You win. And I shall check to see how many spelling mistakes you make.' She was sorry to be doing anything that was likely to upset anyone, but she was going to make the most of the few days she had outside the convent, so when she was back behind those solid walls again she would have a rich store of memories to sustain her. She would do penance for her frivolities, but she would never regret them.

★   ★   ★

'Guess what! You know we were both due to fly home in eight days' time?'

'Yes . . . '

'The tourist office told me they had a couple of cancellations for tomorrow. We've finished our work here, and it's terribly hot.

29

How about us both going back tomorrow? We could spend the rest of our time together in green and beautiful England.'

Rosie hesitated. She could hardly stay in the same place as Bill, yet she would hate to return to the convent so early. All this freedom was now, literally, a chance in a lifetime and she would love to be able to see her mother in Wales. 'Would they change the tickets?'

'Oh yes, the travel people here are much more accommodating than our lot.' Rosie's anxiety was clear to see, 'Don't look so worried. You needn't report back to your office, wherever you work, until your time is up.'

Sister Mary Rose believed that the good had some bad in them and the bad had some good; she hadn't yet decided what sort of a mixture Bill Oldham was. 'Are you married?'

'Good heavens no. Are you?'

She shook her head and wondered what he would say if she told him that she was married to God.

'I have never been to London, have you?'

'No.'

'So let's do it. We've got eight whole days.'

Rose's mind was in a whirl. 'We'd be on the same flight?'

'We'd be sitting together and there are no

snags, no extra charges. Apparently so many people want to stay on here they'll have no trouble selling our tickets, so it'll be a straight swap.'

She mopped her brow. 'This heat really is exhausting. Yes, I would like to come, too. I've heard that there are a great many churches in London — the people living in a city like that must all be very good.'

Bill grinned. 'Right then, pack your things. The plane leaves from Dubrovnik at ten tomorrow morning, so it will mean an early start.'

★ ★ ★

After he had gone she flopped into an armchair and tried to think. She knew so little about men. Apart from her father and one or two school teachers, and of course the old gardener at St. John's, she had very little to do with them at all. Jesus was a man . . . and she had always been close to him. Come to think of it she had spoken to Jesus more than anybody else.

She wondered about Bill Oldham. He was nice, but he looked a rather rough unbelieving type. Maybe she should talk to him. Maybe God had arranged this meeting so that she should try and convert him.

31

She looked at herself in the long mirror. Mirrors had been forbidden in the convent. The nuns had not been allowed to look at their reflection anywhere, not even in a pool of rainwater. Her face, which a few days ago had been deathly pale, was now sunburnt. Her hair was still terribly short, but there were hardly any grey hairs. Incredible at thirty-eight years of age. Those twenty years, instead of ageing her, had left her fairly young-looking. True, she was inclined to frown and her mouth looked a little grim after all those years of austerity and obedience, but her eyes were wide and clear. She was slim, too, which surprised her. The heavy gown for all its dignity had made her feel perpetually fat, like a parcel without the string to hold it all together. In reality, the years of good plain convent food and hard physical exercise in the vegetable garden had slimmed her down nicely.

She pulled herself together. Vanity again! Already that mirror was undermining the very fabric of her calling: loosening the knot that tied her vows. Furthermore, the days had gone so quickly that she hardly had time to read her Day Office. London ... The immensity of Bill's plan made her feel bewildered and a little afraid.

They met again in one of the little cafés for

supper. Bill arrived waving their tickets in the air, 'I've got them! We fly tomorrow.'

The finality of this arrangement left her even more nervous. There had been moments when the sudden release from St. John's, combined with meeting Bill, had seemed like a wild dream. At all costs, she had told herself, she must never break her vows; never throw away those twenty years as if they had been so much chaff to the wind. They had worked hard on her project and, if she had completed it early what harm was there in spending those last few days among the people, good and bad, for whom she had been praying for all those years? And there was always the comforting thought that she would have the rest of her life at St. John's with which to come to terms with any misdemeanour, which she might, unwittingly, have made.

★   ★   ★

Bill had been wrapped in thought, too. For ten years he had been totally deprived of everything that came naturally to a man. He had met this lovely woman and he had been struggling with the temptations, which had been bottled up inside him for so many years, and which only the fear of God helped him to

33

overcome. In many ways he longed to be back on that windswept rock. There he knew where he stood, and where his soul was safe. He thought of London, and eight whole days with Rosie — he knew that he had to go. But where could they stay? He knew no-one in the city, had no kith or kin nearby.

A religious hostel? He remembered the literature that periodically arrived at St. Joseph's. This hostel never gave up its efforts to convert the sinners of this world, and even the monks in their faraway stronghold were not excluded from their mail-shots. For was it not against the laws of nature, and therefore a bad thing, for groups of men to be shut away among themselves for life when God's whole purpose had been for men and women to live together?

'Let's stay in a Christian hostel I know of.' He told her all about it.

'Yes, I have heard of it.' Rose said with obvious relief.

Would this woman ever fail to surprise him? Bill had no way of knowing that St. John's Abbey was included on the hostel's mailing list. Bill Oldham was pleased to have put her at her ease; she would be in good hands if they stayed there.

★　★　★

34

Rosie felt a little guilty when they boarded the coach for the airport next morning, rather like running away from school. And she sensed the same emotion in Bill. But why? She had finished her report. There were only eight days left, and what were a few days in a lifetime? There would be problems, of course. The hostel might be full up. And they had little ready cash between them. Rosie hadn't given it much thought, she was so used to having everything arranged and provided. Bill had told her that they would stay at the hostel, and because it was a religious institution she had not been unduly worried.

When the plane took off with that frightening blast, which she remembered so vividly, she felt as if she had left some of herself behind in Yugoslavia and she felt a happier, more restless spirit take hold. Bill, too, looked happy. Maybe flying up there in the clouds had something to do with it . . .

The plane was still gaining height and the sea was spread out below them like fused glass. Rosie remembered Rockensand and how close the Abbey was to the sea. Sometimes she would catch a glimpse of it from her cell window. And she would lie awake at night and listen to the surf, that same sea, which seemed to cover the entire world down there beneath them.

The stewardess came round with the drinks trolley, but Rosie shook her head. She did not want a drink.

'Not even a glass of wine? Why, Jesus's first miracle was to change water into wine.' Bill went on to quote from Ecclesiasticus: ''Wine is as good as life to a man, if it be drunk moderately; what is life then to a man that is without wine? For it was made to make men glad.''

Rosie was surprised that Bill Oldham, who seemed a rough farming type, could quote so readily from the scriptures, and before she could stop him he had tipped some into her glass. She had only tasted it at Communion before . . . this wine was rich and full-bodied and tasted exactly the same. It seemed to relax her and she closed her eyes and let her mind drift back to her youth and the convent near her home in Wales. The Mass she had attended there seemed a long, long time ago.

She had sat with the villagers at the back of the little chapel: the silence, the comforting little red lamp, which seemed to burn forever, the solemn chanting, she had loved all that. She remembered a lone novice, her white veil the emblem of purity in that dimmed chapel; how the light in her eyes seemed to mirror the devotion of one who was about to dedicate the rest of her life to God. Rosie had

wanted all that, too, and if her life held
another sixty or seventy years, what was that
compared to eternity? Better to spend it all
with God now, from the word go.

The plane gave a lurch and she came to
with a start. Suppose the plane were to crash?
A punishment for her sins! And she was a
sinner, wasn't she? Not returning to the
Abbey when her project was finished. Going
off with this Bill Oldham?

She wondered whether to look upon the
wine as a sort of last Communion. If the
plane fell, would 35,000 feet give her time to
say her prayers?

3

Bill was enjoying Rosie's company; he tried to work out how they could stay together for the remaining eight days. He would take her on a tour of London and see all the famous places — and he could take lots of photographs. Would she like that or would she rather see the open countryside? He was a little puzzled about Rosie. Was she really a schoolteacher or a journalist . . . something professional like that? Her voice was soft and there was a peace about her, which seemed to suggest something else . . .

'You wait here, I'll go and ring the hostel.'

'Don't be long, Bill.'

He could not fail to notice the lack of self-confidence in this beautiful, innocent woman. There was no way she was in a profession that involved dealing with the public! Why couldn't he just ask her what she did for a living? But then she would ask the same of him . . .

★ ★ ★

Rosie waited patiently on a bench. The crowds she had seen here at Heathrow, before, looked the same now. Haggard faces, staring eyes, nobody smiling, nobody happy. A man came and sat next to her. She looked about anxiously. Where had Bill got to? Had this hostel idea been just a lot of talk? Had he gone for good?

'Need a lift? I've got a car outside. Save you on taxis!' He was small and shifty, and he scared her in a way she had not felt before, at least not while in the convent. But before she had time to worry about how to get rid her predator, she heard Bill's reassuring call, 'Rosie, I telephoned the hostel. We're lucky. They are keeping a couple of single rooms for us!'

Thank goodness. After all, she knew little enough about Bill and she wasn't too naïve to know that she needed to be wise in her dealings with men!

★　★　★

They travelled to the East End by Underground. It was rush hour, people scurried about — automatons on the routine journey home. Yet they looked scared and miserable. Bill and Rosie hung on for dear life as the train thundered through the tunnel as if it was bound for hell itself. The train slammed to a stop. The doors opened and people pressed in, pushing and shoving, while others tried to get out before the door closed again trapping them in this infernal capsule.

Bill became separated from Rosie. He could see her squashed up against the opposite door with another man's rough face too close to her gentle cheeks. He was leering at her. How dare this ape treat his Rosie with such overt crudity! Bill felt helpless and angry. He could do nothing without causing a major scene, and he judged this would cause Rosie even more distress.

There was a sickening smell of garlic. Rose couldn't move, Bill could read the feelings of entrapment in her features. She seemed scared to put her weight on the door. Did she not know that this door would not open onto the track at each station, or was she afraid the weight of all those people would cause it to fly open? She was leaning towards the other passengers, sending out all the wrong messages to the predatory males aboard. Could they not see how innocent she was?

A clergyman fought his way on board. Probably a good and kind person as a rule, but here he was pushing and shoving to get into the compartment like everybody else. Nobody smiled. Bill thought about the wide-open spaces of the world and wondered why they all did it.

It was raining when they got off the train and Bill felt sorry for Rosie. He could tell she was exhausted and it was he who had dragged her away from Yugoslavia. 'If you'd rather call it a day and go home I'll come with you, Rosie, and see you off on the train.'

Slowly her face relaxed. She smiled, but said nothing. Bill dared to hope she didn't want to leave him just like that. Home! Where was home to her? Would she take him there one day? Maybe there would be time . . . He would put off going back to the monastery until the last possible moment. The remaining eight days in the outside world would be ten times better for his soul than back there.

Outside tall buildings shut out most of the light from the dark grey sky. People were still hurrying home. Umbrellas everywhere. Full busses pulled into full gutters, splashing unwary pedestrians waiting impatiently for their turn to escape the misery of the persistent rain.

An old man, shabbily dressed, sat on the steps outside the station, his cap on the slab beside him. The wet weather didn't seem to bother him. He simply picked up his cap and tipped out the water.

41

'What about you, Bill? Do you want to go home?'

Bill could hear the other brothers: 'Back so early when you had the chance of a lifetime to see something of the outside world?' And they would be right. Come to think of it he was not much better than a prisoner, a lifer, who had been given a two-week parole.

★   ★   ★

They arrived at the hostel looking wet and dishevelled. Their knock was answered by a tall, kindly woman. She greeted them with the same welcoming smile she gave all newcomers, especially down-and-outs. Miss Hopkins considered herself to be a mind reader as well as a saver of souls, and through her doors had passed every kind of human flotsam. She had seen it all and from her no secrets were hidden.

'Are you married?'

Bill shook his head, while Rosie's colour deepened.

'I am Bill Oldham and this is Mary Rose.'

'Have you both sinned and fallen short of the love of God?'

'I don't think so,' Rosie stuttered.

'Not me,' was Bill's spirited reply.

42

Miss Hopkins shook her head. Why did people always deny their sins? These two had obviously been living together and the only mitigating thing about them was that they were not drunk. She smiled again and took them inside. 'It is quite clear to me that Jesus has sent you both here to be saved. Now in your rooms you will each find a Bible,' she broke off and stared at them. 'Have either of you ever read the Bible?'

Before Rosie could reply Bill gave one of his cheeky boyish smiles: 'I did see a copy once, and I liked the pictures inside.'

'There are no pictures in our Bibles,' Miss Hopkins grew more serious. 'We put them in the rooms, because we expect them to be read. And I suggest you both read the Revelation of St. John The Divine, Chapter Twenty before you go to bed tonight.'

At that moment Bill was more concerned about money. 'When I rang up I should have asked how much you charge for B&B.'

'The only charge we make is upon your souls, but in exchange for your board and lodging we would like you both to accompany us on one of our local missions.'

'Missions?'

'Yes. We hold services in the streets and we also visit the public houses and the homes for the destitute. We would like you both to accompany one of our ladies into a public house tomorrow evening, so that she is not left entirely on her own. There have been one or two nasty incidents lately, due, no doubt, to the corrupt state of our society. One of our ladies was assaulted in Stepney recently.'

'I am so sorry. What happened, was she all right?'

Miss Hopkins hesitated, took Bill aside and said something to him in a low voice.

Their rooms overlooked a dismal courtyard where two scruffy men — the rest of the day's catch — were sitting on a bench smoking cigarettes. Lost sheep, which had been found, and soon, hopefully, would be saved.

Sitting at the long wooden tables they ate baked beans, eggs and chips, followed by strong sweet tea, all served by a prim, yet joyful, hostel woman. For were they not like Christ? That's what the notice across the entrance said: All Visitors To Be Received As Christ.

It was an uneasy night. Groans and curses came from rooms further along the corridor. One man repeatedly shouted out the same dreadful swearword. Rosie heard Bill go along the passage to tell him to keep quiet.

The next day they were free until the evening when they were expected to help with the mission work. In the Abbey Rosie had been trying to save souls by proxy, as it were. Out here she would have to mix with the sort of people she had been praying for. She would see people as Jesus saw them. Neither He nor any of his disciples ever shut themselves away in monasteries!

Rosie tried not to think of it, but the nagging thought wouldn't go away, and she took comfort by remembering her vows. By making those solemn promises to God she had chained herself to St. John's Abbey, away from the outside world, because she had believed this was what God had wanted her to do.

The day was hot and sunny and they opted for a tour of the city outskirts on top of a bus. In the afternoon, Bill and Rosie were relieved to get away from it all into St. James's Park. Rosie mused, 'How depressing it must be to live in such places, Bill.'

'Poor souls. I wonder if they ever get to enjoy the countryside.'

Rosie wished she had the courage to ask him where he came from. But then he would have returned her enquiry and she was not ready to break the spell . . .

★   ★   ★

45

Happy and content in each other's company, they sat on a park bench, both trying to remember when they had last seen a lake with ornamental ducks. Rosie looked along the path at the next group of people to pass by and gasped. Coming towards them, in full regalia, was the Reverend Mother herself! Rosie remembered that she had been due to go to London for some big ecclesiastical meeting at a religious hall. And here she was, coming ever closer . . . 'Why hasn't she recognised me? It must be my civilian clothes.'

In panic, Rosie turned, buried her head in Bill's chest and threw her arms around him. When it was safe again, she sat back, her face red. 'It was somebody I would rather not see. Somebody who thinks I should still be in Yugoslavia . . . '

Bill looked up and down the towpath. 'Well, there was only that old nun and she's gone now.' He grinned. 'You've got a novel way of playing hide and seek!'

The park was a good place to be, an oasis in a concrete jungle, and they lingered there until late in the afternoon. Then back to the Underground and the fast moving escalators. The rush hour. Teeming millions. People going up. People going down. Why didn't they think to avoid it!

Back at the hostel Miss Hopkins looked them over, and tried unsuccessfully to sniff discreetly, to see if they had been drinking. She was surprised when she learned that they had been touring London and looking at historical buildings. Very few of her inmates were scholarly people; most of them spent their time looking for a good place to spread out their cardboard, and all they could boast about were the best bridges to sleep under, or where the warm air ventilators were situated. These two, though down on their luck, did seem to be a cut above the others. 'When you two registered with us you didn't say what your occupations were.'

★ ★ ★

Bill Oldham hesitated. If he told Miss Hopkins he was a monk, she would think he was also trying to be funny. And, even if she believed him, she had a right to be upset. What could be worse than a monk taking advantage of a legitimate reason to spend time in the outside world to pick up a woman — an obviously naïve one at that! Talk about the devil at work! Better to leave the hostel and find rooms where nobody cared who they were. Better, by far, to avoid religious places and live among the easy-come easy-go general population! 'We're both out of work,' Bill said bluntly.

Miss Hopkins understood. Lots of people were out of work!

'Have either of you ever done any work for God?'

Bill shook his head. 'Not much.'

She looked at Rosie. 'Oh, just a little. You know, here and there.'

'Here and there? Well, would you both like to come along tonight and do a little more for Him? Could you be back here at seven o'clock?'

Beatrice was a fat, smiling girl whose eyes had seen the glory of the coming of the Lord, and Bill and Rosie were to accompany her to a riverside pub — The Ship at High Tide. It was Saturday night and the place was crowded with local people and dockside workers. Beatrice told them that she often visited the pub alone, but on Saturday nights she tried to get somebody to go with her.

'I heard about you being attacked.'

'Yes, luckily some dockers were doing a late shift and they came to my rescue. Most people like the hostel, even if we do stand for preaching and spoiling their fun. Anyway, the police were called, but I didn't prefer any charges.'

'Why not?'

'Because you should turn the other cheek!'

She was glad they were going along with her, Bill Oldham looked big enough to stand up to anybody at The Ship. They took up position just inside the entrance, and while Beatrice read from the Bible Rosie and Bill distributed her leaflets. The manager behind the bar knew Beatrice, but he gave Bill and Rosie a look, which said, 'What the hell are you doing here if you're not drinking!'

People came up and spoke to Beatrice. One or two drinks and they were ready to pour out all their troubles. She listened patiently and talked to them about God, and offered to call at their homes to try and settle their disputes.

★   ★   ★

Beatrice, left alone to do her thing, could probably save more souls than a whole monastery of monks, Bill decided. There were so many people packed into such a small and smoky place. And they were restless, waiting for an excuse to explode, and the shouting and brawling, the utter hopelessness of it all, reminded him of something he had read in a story by Dante. When Beatrice disappeared, a couple of skinheads came up to them. Bill had never seen a skinhead; he thought they were clowns, dressed up to do some stunt for the pub.

'Want a drink?'

Bill shook his head and declined politely.

'What the hell are you doing in here if you're not drinking then?'

'We're helping the girl from the hostel.'

That was like a red rag to a bull. One of the skinheads thrust his glass right under Bill's nose, spilling beer over his clothes. 'Don't try and be funny with me, now drink, I insist!'

Bill Oldham, who had survived on that rock of his for ten years, wasn't afraid of anybody or anything. Indeed, like many monks who have been confined for long periods in monasteries, he was imbued with a pretty tough streak. 'I told you, we don't want a drink.'

He dodged the fist, which followed, and punched the skinhead hard in the stomach. His companion produced a bicycle chain, but before he could do anything with it Bill had wrenched it out of his hands. The heavy chain knocked over some beer glasses and ended up in the lap of a young tough sitting at the next table. There was uproar. Everybody was shouting and shoving. The landlord, unable to maintain order, rang for the police.

Bill managed to get Rosie outside, but the

shrieking and scuffling continued until the police arrived. The skinheads vanished while Bill and Rosie were left to face the angry landlord and his customers.

'They started the whole thing. They came into my pub and just hung about as if they wanted to nick something!' The landlord pointed at Bill. 'He started to punch one of my customers!'

Everybody, including the police, were good customers at the pub and were on the landlord's side. Complete strangers, stood little chance.

Bill looked around, 'Where is Beatrice? She'll tell you we are with her.'

'Here! Yes, that's right. They are staying at the hostel and have come to help me,' she tried to explain.

'As if we believe that. We're not daft. You're just doing your Holy Jo bit again!' One of them leered at Bill. 'Trying to shelter under a religious skirt, wimp?'

★   ★   ★

Rosie and Bill were bundled into a van and driven to the police station where they were charged with insulting behaviour and disturbing the peace. They were given a meal and then put into adjoining cells and told that they would appear before the magistrates in the morning.

Bill could see the sky through the little barred window. The cell contained bed, table, chair . . . and a bible . . . a glimmer of hope.

'If I ascend to heaven you are there,

if I make my bed in Sheol you are there . . . '

He discovered that he was able to talk to Rosie in the next cell, and once during the night he was surprised to hear her say her rosary. He hadn't realised that she was religious. Bill tried to reassure himself that St. Paul had once been in prison, but he found little comfort in it. To be locked up without any chance of immediately proving your innocence was one of the worst human conditions.

4

Next morning Bill was conducted into the courtroom and arraigned before an august-looking woman in glasses who was seated between two elderly men. The usual sort of people occupied the public gallery: the press, members of the public, hangers-on who had nothing better to do — all who wanted something to talk about, especially if there was anything of a sadistic nature. And, of course, Beatrice was there, too, looking very sorrowful.

Beatrice was a familiar figure in the courthouse: she would defend anybody, even those who were guilty of the worst crimes. And her presence in that courtroom was often the cause of some lighter sentence.

The portly JP looked over her glasses at Bill. 'You are charged with disturbing the peace and causing an affray at the public house known as The Ship at High Tide last night. What have you to say? Are you guilty or not guilty?'

She would have used the same tone of voice if she had been addressing a murderer, and Bill wondered what awful crime he had committed to be brought here and treated like any common criminal. Making friends with Rosie? Was that a crime? And was God now about to punish him for it?

'Well?'

Bill explained that he was a monk on leave from St. Joseph's Abbey and he described how he had met Rosie in Medjugorje and they had travelled back to England together. How in exchange for lodging at the hostel they had agreed to help with mission work and had accompanied Beatrice to the local inn; Beatrice had disappeared and Bill, who had been assaulted by a skinhead, had merely defended himself while trying to get Rosie out of the place.

A monk indeed! A titter went round the courtroom, while Beatrice sat there, her head bowed, as if in prayer.

The landlord was in court, together with several of his customers, and their evidence was overwhelming. Bill was found guilty and fined £20 — almost all the money he had in the world.

Bill was hurried away.

★　★　★

Rosie was brought into the dock.

'Name?'

'Mary Rose.'

'Occupation?'

'I am a nun.'

The magistrate put her pen down and looked round at her two colleagues in despair, while Beatrice sank her head into even deeper prayer.

'Don't try and be funny!' the magistrate warned her.

'But I am a nun,' and Rosie, close to tears, told her story.

'I am very sorry about all this.'

The magistrate sat back. A nun indeed! She had seen some strange people in the dock before, but she had never heard of anybody claiming to be a nun.

'You are charged with disturbing the peace. Are you guilty or not guilty?'

Rosie did not seem to understand. She shook her head and said nothing. The magistrate guessed she had been thrown out of her convent. A nun, put out into the street! Better not to have become a nun in the first place. Better to have faced the world outside like any other wretched human being!

'Your home, then, where do you live?'

Rosie could only gulp and gaze helplessly at those frowning faces. 'I am staying in a religious hostel.' She named the place.

The magistrate looked across at Beatrice who nodded.

'If you really are a nun then I advise you to return to your convent. Ask them to give you one more chance, because, believe me, you will find no peace out here!' She studied her notes and then looked up. 'Because you have apologised to us and you are apparently in the care of this hostel, I will fine you only ten pounds!'

Rosie, was unable to stop her tears, 'I am sorry, but I lost my purse last night and I have no money!'

The magistrate, who had a whole list of cases to deal with that morning, shook her head and spoke to her two colleagues. Finally she looked at Rosie. 'Case dismissed. You are free to go, but I warn you . . . don't let me see you in here again!'

★   ★   ★

Rosie came out of the Magistrates Court looking pale and drawn. Bill was waiting. He was glad that they had appeared in the dock separately; the secret of his occupation was still safe. He began to wonder how long he could keep on pretending that he was just an ordinary person. Was he committing a grave sin by this continuing deception? Wasn't it

56

time he told Rosie who he was, said goodbye, and made tracks for his monastery on the island of Toy?

'I am sorry, it is all my fault!' he said miserably. 'I suppose we had better move on and go our separate ways. Although I must admit I was beginning to enjoy our friendship together.'

She sat down on a wall. Following her courtroom ordeal Rosie seemed far away — lost in thought — as though she were sorting out something deep within herself.

He really did not know what to do for the best . . . If he were to leave her now he would feel lonely. Could he cope without her? Should he drag himself back to the rock and monastic life? He rarely prayed for himself, but at this time he needed to know what His Father wanted of him.

Rosie broke into his thoughts, 'If you are in no hurry to get back then come with me to Wales and meet my mother . . . ' The words came in a rush before she could think properly. 'We could walk the hills and explore the countryside together. Wales is beautiful!'

Bill studied her face. She was happy. And so, he realised, was he. 'There's one small thing.' She turned her head to one side, and trustingly — childlike — she looked up into his face. 'Money! After paying the fine I've only got about fifteen pounds left!'

How could he explain that he had such a small amount of money? People who travelled about and went to places like Yugoslavia had chequebooks and bank accounts, and they could go and draw out cash. Monks had nothing except the clothes they stood up in and even his civilian clothing had been on loan. Only fifteen pounds. Rosie must think he was a pretty down-and-out type.

'And I lost my purse last night and couldn't pay my fine.'

It never occurred to Bill to wonder why she was so strapped for cash.

Rosie stuck out her chin, 'I shall go to Wales and see my mother even if I have to walk there!'

Bill had not seen this determined streak in her. If asked he would have described her as rather submissive.

'At least that fifteen pounds would help you to start back home again,' she continued.

'What, and leave you here alone, down-and-out, in London?' Bill shook his head. 'No. We sink or swim together. Look, I've got some time left and I have never been to Wales. I'd love to come and meet your mother. How about it, shall we stick together?' Bill could not lose her now. 'Look, the sun's come out and it's going to be a wonderful day. Let's go back to the hostel and pack our things. And then try and hitchhike to Wales.'

★ ★ ★

Beatrice had already reported the court's findings to Miss Hopkins. 'We are not an institution for the righteous, but a house for sinners and you will always be welcome here!'

★ ★ ★

Bill and Rosie stood by the motorway and waited for a lift. Twenty years ago green fields would have stretched as far as the eye could see. Now cars whizzed past them like bullets.

A big truck drew up. 'I can take you as far as Newbury,' the driver offered. 'That's where I have to unload this stuff.'

They had hoped to go further than that, but at least it was in the right direction, and better than another long wait by the roadside; they climbed up beside him.

'Where're you heading for?'

'Wales. It's a little place called Treriver.'

'Can't say I've heard of it. Sounds as if you've got a long way to go!'

The driver dropped them on the slip road off the A34 roundabout, before turning off to

Newbury, and Bill and Rosie decided to avoid the motorway and get a lift along one of the country lanes, which led westward. After the din of the motorway a great peace descended: the road seemed to wind on into the green countryside forever. For Bill it was all wonderful, and he marvelled at the rich, fertile soil spread out on either side. 'Where I come from there are no trees or green fields and if you want to grow anything you have to bring the soil in from somewhere and then add fertiliser.'

'No trees?'

'Too windswept and salty and we have to work very hard to grow anything at all.'

'Where do you live? Sounds as if you are close to the sea.'

'I live on an island . . . ' He stopped.

'An island? How exciting. I have always wanted to live on an island!'

Bill shrugged and said nothing.

★   ★   ★

Rosie could not hide from herself any longer that Bill was just as unwilling to talk about his job and home as she was. Maybe it was some small inconspicuous island, which was connected to the mainland by a causeway, or a bridge . . . or marshland. Not a proper island in fact. Like the Isle of Purbeck, for instance. She decided to bring it up some other time.

They had been following the same winding country road for nearly an hour when they saw a campfire in the trees, and a tramp getting ready for the night. They went across and asked him how far it was to the nearest village. 'You'll never make it. There's no lighting on this road and there's no moon tonight. You'd be better off going back the way you came.'

He was a well-built man, tanned and bearded, with a good accent, and Bill guessed that, hard driven by some wind of chance, he had walked out on his life. 'Thorndyke's the name. You can spend the night here if you like. Sleep out under the stars for a change, and then you and your wife can hop a lift on the milk van in the morning.'

'We're not married,' Bill said.

Thorndyke shrugged and said nothing.

★　★　★

They learned that Thorndyke was single, and had once had a career in the city. 'The financial rewards were fantastic, but the cost was just too much. I knew deep down that all the creature comforts that job gave me were

61

not enough. And I feared that if I stayed I would end up in a mental hospital — burnt out and depressed.'

'What are you doing wandering the by-ways?' Bill asked jovially.

'I decided there was more to life and decided to sell up, leave the city and take to the open road.'

Bill and Rosie listened sympathetically, 'Will you ever go back to it?'

'No. I have learned more out here beneath these stars than in all my years in an office. Things I never gave a second thought to years ago — is there anything after this life . . . ? Are we on our own . . . ?'

Bill had wondered about those stars, too. How often on the island of Toy had he looked up at that vast panoply and tried to reason things out. But those stars, so high above the Atlantic, had told him nothing, and he had come to the conclusion that everything that mattered was here, on this earth: life and death, and especially death.

Thorndyke broke into his muses, 'As far as I am concerned, understanding the hereafter is like trying to play chess when you don't even know the rules.'

'Your sort of life is all very well in summer,' Bill was ever practical, 'but what on earth do you do in winter?'

'I could rent somewhere, but it doesn't appeal to me now. I spend the winters in Wales. The foresters leave their huts empty and I go to a little place in the Black Mountains. It lies in a deep valley, sheltered from the weather. I read all the books I have ever wanted to and I get my food from the village shop.'

Rosie remembered the valley; 'It's not far from Treriver. It's a well-known beauty spot with streams of rushing water and flowers, even during the winter.' She reached out to touch Bill's hand, 'I'll take you there, it's not far from my home. They say that if you toss a coin into one of those streams your wish will come true!'

'My wish came true that very day we met on the mountain, Rosie.' Maybe it was the colour of the sunset, or the deep stillness about them, but he had wanted to say something like that for a long time. All he wanted was to put his arms round her slender waist; silently he cursed, because Thorndyke was there.

★ ★ ★

They enjoyed an outdoor barbecue supper with Thorndyke and listened to stories of his high-flyer life before he left the rat race, until wet dew reminded them that another day was at hand.

The next morning, with the arrival of the milk van, they said their goodbyes.

'I shall be going to Wales again soon, so maybe we'll meet up again!'

5

At the next big town Bill gave Rosie some money and she tried to telephone her mother. The telephone system had changed over the years and she had difficulty in getting through. When at last a strange voice answered, she thought she had got the wrong number.

'This is a neighbour, my dear. I am sorry, but your mother has had an accident. She fell and broke her hip; she has had to go into hospital . . . '

Rosie was overcome with fear. Her mother was all she had in the world. Hospital! She was almost beside herself in that prison of a telephone box. 'When did this happen?'

'Five days ago. I live next door, and I have been tidying up the house and dealing with the tradesmen. I happened to be there when your call came through . . . '

Rosie interrupted her. 'How is she now? How bad is she?'

'I am sorry, but I am afraid she has been very ill with pneumonia . . . We tried to contact you at St. John's, but the Reverend Mother said you had gone to Yugoslavia. She tried to get in touch with you over there, but there was no telephone where you were staying, and nobody seemed to know where you were. And then a couple of days ago the airline said you had returned to England.'

In that stifling telephone box Rosie wanted to be sick. So it was a punishment! Oh, God, not my mother! She told the woman that she was already on her way home and that she would go straight to the hospital.

Bill did his best to comfort her, but Rosie, distraught, ran into the road waving her arms. A car pulled up suddenly. 'What's wrong, are you tired of life?'

'I must get to Wales . . . to the hospital . . . my mother has had a serious accident.'

'What part of Wales?'

'It's a little place called Treriver.'

'Hop in. I'm going to Wales and I'll run you up there, and drop you off at the hospital.'

During the journey Rosie wondered whether she could obtain leave of absence from the convent in order to look after her mother. This, she knew, would not be easy; she would be told that God came first and that she could do more for her mother by prayer in their little chapel. She remembered that other sisters who had wanted to visit sick or ageing relatives were hardly ever granted leave. They were an enclosed order and the regulations had been made clear to them from the start.

In other words all healing of the sick was to be carried out by round the clock prayers in the precincts of the convent, and God would either cure or not cure according to His will. Having been granted special permission to leave the convent for the purpose of visiting Medjugorje, Rosie thought she stood a good chance of extending her absence in order to take care of her mother, and found some notepaper and started on a rough draft:

'Dear Reverend Mother,

I was on my way back from Yugoslavia when I was informed, sadly, that my mother had been taken ill . . . '

If she told the whole truth: that she had met a man called Bill Oldham and they had been involved in a spot of bother together in an East End pub, and had then appeared in court, the Reverend Mother would have believed that Satan had dragged one of her daughters into the Bottomless Pit. Surely, Rose asked herself, it must be a good thing — sometimes — for Christians to hide a bit of the truth? And yet, deep down, she knew that if she kept her vows she should tell the Reverend Mother everything.

And there was another nagging thought.

Leave of absence. How long would that be? A few days, a week at the most? A fractured hip, followed by pneumonia, could take a long time to recover from . . . And her mother couldn't possibly afford help in the house. How could she return to the convent and leave her alone and ill?

She remembered that part of her vows: 'You will remain in the precincts of St. John's Abbey in the face of all earthly trials and tribulations, obedient, surrendering your whole mind, body and soul to Almighty God until death.'

Her mother was very ill. Why didn't they allow for things like that in those vows? She did not need to ask herself what Jesus would have done.

Bill did his best to cheer her up. 'Lots of people break their hip. The surgeons are marvellous with things like that these days. Your mother will be up and about again in no time!'

The driver took them straight to the hospital, 'Thank you so much, I can see my mother first and then go to the shops for anything she needs.'

'You're welcome, only too glad to help.' And with that he was gone.

★ ★ ★

The hospital, a Victorian monstrosity modernised inside, had been built mostly for casualties from the coalmines. Bill and Rosie were shown into the waiting room. The receptionist telephoned the ward and after about ten minutes a young doctor entered the room. He would not meet her gaze; Rosie could tell that something was wrong. He glanced down at the file in his hands and then he looked round at the ward sister who had come up behind him, before turning to Rosie. 'I am sorry to have to tell you that your mother passed away peacefully about two hours ago . . . '

Rosie would have collapsed if Bill had not been there. He put his arms round her and eased her into a chair.

'It was the pneumonia. She died without pain. She fell asleep peacefully.'

Rosie felt a sudden hatred for this man whose words seemed to pound her brain like a sledgehammer. Her mother was dead!

All she wanted was to get out of there and run so far this awful news could not catch up with her; across those Welsh hills and disappear into that blue sky forever.

'Your mother is in the mortuary. Would you like to see her?' asked the ward sister.

'No, I do not want to see my mother in a mortuary. I have come all this way to see her alive, not dead.' No, she didn't want to see her mother laid out on some mortuary slab. She would rather remember her as she was, a wonderfully kind person and the best mother of them all.

The ward sister did her best to comfort her, but she was also very busy and made her excuses for getting back to the ward. Before she left she handed Rosie an envelope. 'Your mother left this for you.'

Rosie stuffed the envelope into her pocket and tried to choke back her tears. Bill, almost overcome with shock by what had happened, took her gently by the hand and led her away.

She left the hospital stunned and ashamed, with the realisation that had she reported directly to the convent on her return from Yugoslavia, she might have had time to see her mother while she was still alive. Clearly the wrath of God had descended. She was so distraught, nothing seemed to matter any more; she decided to tell Bill Oldham she was a nun of the Benedictine Order.

★ ★ ★

Seen through her tear-filled eyes, the pretty little cottage seemed to quiver. Her heart ached to see all the curtains closed; her memories were of happier times with her mother, how she loved to spend time in the beautiful garden tending her precious plants. 'I'm nearer to God here than anywhere, dear.' Even with the cotton curtains drawn, out of respect for the dead, there was a strong sense of peace about the place.

Not for her mother the ritual ceremonies of religion; she talked to her Lord as if He were there beside her as she worked. Rosie could still hear her singing her favourite hymn . . . 'What a friend we have in Jesus . . . ' 'What do I need all that incense and stuff for, dear, when I have the scent of His creation to lift my spirits here at home.'

Her mother never had any doubts about where she would spend eternity. Not for her penances ordered by the Reverend Mother. She simply *knew* that there was nothing for her to do, but to live her faith every day. 'Don't you worry, I know Jesus loves me and has a place in heaven waiting for me when the time comes . . . ' And now the time had come. There would be the funeral arrangements, bills to pay, and letters to write. She decided to write to the Reverend Mother rather than telephone, because this would give her more time. But there was always the nagging thought that she would be told to return to the convent immediately, because God needed her most.

She had no friends in the village; she had been away for too long. She was glad that Bill was still with her. She dearly hoped that he would stay.

★   ★   ★

Entering the cottage was like revisiting a beautiful dream. The blue and white painted kitchen with its Welsh dresser. The sitting room leading through French windows into the garden. She went upstairs to her bedroom, everything was there, just as it had been all those years ago when her mother used to come in and kiss her goodnight. Fresh tears stung her eyes.

The letter they had given her at the hospital! The letter from her mother! With trembling hands she opened the envelope and stared at the writing, so weak, so irregular . . .

'Dear Rosie,

'Please try and be brave for what I am about to tell you. I am afraid that I have been taken very ill and I am writing this in hospital. The people at St. John's Abbey have been trying to contact you, but without success. They have all been very kind to me here and everything possible has been done, but I feel now that the end is close at hand.

'If I do not come home again, my dear Rosie, never forget how much I love you. Forgive me when I tried to dissuade you from taking your vows, for I have long since believed that what you did in those far off days was right and wonderful in the sight of God.

'Rosie, do not say goodbye. Love is stronger than death and I know that one day God will bring us together again.

'Mother.'

'Rosie! Tea's ready!'

Rosie tried to dry her tears. She drew back the curtains and opened the window, but even the cool breeze did nothing to calm her. She remembered that when she still lived at home she kept her powder compact and lipstick in the small drawer under her dressing-table mirror; it was still there. She studied herself in the mirror and dabbed some powder on her face. She stared at the lipstick container. Should she? Dare she? Bill was calling again and in a moment he would be on the stairs. She pulled the lipstick out — it looked as good as new. She tried the tiniest of smears; the bright red colour seemed to stand out like a streak of paint on her freshly powdered face. The make-up made her feel distinctly odd, but it was too late to wipe it all off, and she went downstairs.

Bill was examining one of the pictures on the mantelpiece. A neatly framed photograph of Rosie taken with a group of nuns on the day she had completed her vows. 'It's a good picture. Didn't know you at first in all that fancy dress. You must have had fun doing amateur theatricals!'

He just stood there watching her, and Rosie could tell that he knew she had been crying, knew that she had been trying to cover it up with all that make-up. She didn't care. Nothing seemed to matter now that her mother had gone. She suddenly felt abandoned, as if those twenty years of convent life had counted for nothing, and here she was, just like any other poor grieving soul in the outside world. She would probably lose Bill, but how could she keep up this ridiculous pretence any longer?

'Listen, Bill, I really am a nun, and I went to Medjugorje to report on what was happening there. That picture was taken just after my final vows!'

She caught a glimpse of herself in the mirror. A nun? She looked more like one of those street women they all used to pray for!

Bill's jaw dropped, his face revealing the depth of his despair. 'He couldn't be more shocked if I told him I was already married! Which in effect I am.'

In a broken voice he whispered, 'Why didn't you tell me?'

'I kept putting it off. I didn't want to spoil our friendship!'

'But you spoke so passionately about so many things — music . . . art . . . and even politics . . . All that time I thought you were a school teacher!'

She felt his eyes searching her face, as if he were asking for something. 'Join the club! I am a monk!' He thought she would burst out laughing, but the tears were still there and he began to wonder whether they would ever go away. And his side of the story flowed from his lips like an undammed river.

'I didn't tell you that I was a monk, because I thought you'd run a mile!'

Rosie smiled faintly. 'And all the time I thought you were a farmer of some sort,' she stammered. 'I suppose we ought to split up now and go our separate ways!'

'There's no need for that. There's a lot to do here, and I could stay and help you until you've got over all your troubles. After all we've been through together isn't this what Jesus would have wanted us to do?'

★ ★ ★

Bill could tell that Rosie was relieved, but he knew that St. John's would want her to return fairly soon. How could she possibly have enough time to cope with the funeral, and sort out of her mother's affairs — not to mention the sale of the house and contents? Bill thought he could probably take some time off from the monastery. He would write to the Abbot and explain that he was helping somebody who was in trouble . . . He hoped they wouldn't ask too many questions: if he told them it was a nun they would order him back on the next train!

Since meeting Rosie he had been even more enthusiastic about leaving the monastery, and in his wilder moments he had even considered proposing marriage to her. But a nun!

That she would soon disappear out of his life forever was a bitter pill for him to swallow. 'Would you mind if I stayed and helped you sort things out? I am sure I can get some extra time from the Abbot.'

Rosie was pleased. She had nobody in the whole wide world, except Bill. It would be good to have him with her when she had to visit the solicitors and estate agents — and people like that. 'There's plenty of room. You can have the back bedroom, the one that overlooks the garden. We will have to be careful, though. I was brought up here and all the neighbours, everybody in the village, know only too well that I am a nun. So I am afraid there will be some gossip. We will have to tell people that you are just an old friend of the family who is here to help me out, because if anybody discovered that you were a monk there would be a scandal and we'd be in all the papers!'

'A monk and a nun living together?' Bill grinned. 'They'd put us in the village stocks!'

'What do the neighbours expect me to do, put a bed out in the vegetable garden for you? As far as I am concerned having you here in my house as a guest is not committing any sin!'

'Of course it isn't, but some people's minds are like cesspits!' Bill laughed, trying to cheer her up. 'What if we set up a joint monastery and nunnery right here in this house!'

6

The villagers looked curiously at Rosie; many of them remembered the schoolgirl who had become a nun. At first they paid little attention to the rough weather beaten looking man who seemed to be constantly at her side, but as the days passed and he was seen to accompany her on visits to the shops and for long walks in the countryside, they began to wonder what was going on. Rosie, a nun, and rather special in their minds, was not supposed to go about with a man who, they understood, was not related to her.

Tom Yeates, the village postman, looked back from his middle years to the time when he had attended the same school as Mary Rose. If truth be told, he had been rather infatuated by the pretty, reserved little girl whose favourite topic of conversation had seemed to be Jesus. A story he thought it better not to relate to his wife, Betsy.

It was she who brought up the subject on everyone's lips. 'There's something funny going on, if you ask me.' Nobody had, but that would not stop his Betsy. 'She seems to be going out with a rather good looking man.'

Tom grunted from behind his newspaper. This was not a conversation he really wanted to pursue.

'He looks rugged like a seaman, and you know what they're like!'

'He must be an old friend of the family, come down to help her sort things out.' If Tom thought that was going to satisfy his nosey wife he was much mistaken.

'It's not right. A nun, and such a pretty one at that, should have a minder or something . . .'

'She'll be all right.'

'All the same, I don't like it. I was talking to Babs at the milkman's, and she said that Rosie had been seen out in the wilds with this sailor.'

'Let her be, woman. Mary Rose was always a good girl. Strong minded; even though she was quiet. She won't let any man take advantage of her.'

'Really, and how would you know that, Tom Yeates?' Betsy snatched away the newspaper. His blushes exposed, Tom searched his mind for the most appropriate words to pacify his wife.

Much to his relief Betsy was diverted by a knock at the door. 'Come in, Ella.' She stood aside to let the young woman in.

'Who is it?' Not normally interested in

Betsy's gossipy friends, Tom was prepared to welcome anyone with open arms at that moment.

'The policeman's daughter.'

Ella made her way to the cottage kitchen, 'You very kindly invited me to call in for a cuppa and a bun.'

'I did. Come in, my dear, you are most welcome. We were just talking about Sister Mary Rose. I believe you were a couple of years younger than her. At the same school weren't you?'

'I heard. She's back after all these years!' Ella's eyes lit up. 'Her mother died, didn't she. I suppose she'll have to sell up everything before going back to . . . What do they call those places?'

'A convent.' Betsy nodded. 'I don't like the idea of that man being with her all the time.'

Ella's face reddened. 'Some people say he's actually living there — at her cottage.'

'No!'

Tom put his head round the kitchen door and exclaimed brightly, 'What? You mean *living with her?*'

Betsy ignored his remark. She sniffed, 'People do whatever they like these days. You'd think this generation invented sex! Newspapers, the tele, you can't get away from it!'

Ella nodded, 'And most don't bother to get married at all . . . '

Tom thought of the little girl of yesteryear, 'Rosie's OK, though. She's got a pretty face, but there is plenty of character there, more than in a dozen of the villagers around here.'

'Thank you very much!' Betsy snapped. 'Seems to me you have rather a lot to say on the subject of Sister Mary Rose, Tom Yeates. You men are all the same! And you had better be careful not to look at her too long or folks around here will be questioning your intentions — present and past . . . '

Tom grabbed his jacket off his chair. 'Look at the time, I can't stand around here chatting all day, I'm running late. Must get my rounds finished!' And thankfully made his escape.

★   ★   ★

Rosie wrote to the Reverend Mother telling of her bereavement and requesting leave of absence of one month to wind up her mother's affairs. Back came a formal letter of sympathy and the request that Rosie return to the convent within a week, to which Rosie replied respectfully that she could not comply, and would it be possible to obtain a dispensation from Rome in order to allow her the extra time?

81

The reply to this letter was brief. She was granted one month, but if she intended to stay away any longer she would have to seek a dispensation from Rome, and this might well be a lengthy business, which the Reverend Mother would rather avoid.

Rosie noted the severity of the missive, especially considering that it followed her mother's death, and couldn't help wondering if some busybody in the village had reported her association with Bill. The parish priest? Had he written to the Reverend Mother? True, she hadn't attended Mass or been to confession at the little church . . . Anyway, priests were not supposed to give away information, or did that rule only apply to the confessional?

★　★　★

When Rosie called to discuss the arrangements for her mother's funeral the parish priest, Father Connolly, was friendly enough, but he was not like any of the rather staid priests who had called at St. John's Abbey to say Mass. This man wore red corduroy trousers and a brightly coloured open neck shirt. She had seen women dressed like that in London, but never thought to see a man wear such things. Rosie was surprised by her feeling of dislike for him; she had no experience of charismatic churches, and for a moment she wondered whether she had come to the wrong place.

If only she were back behind the safe walls of St. John's Abbey. Out here she was on her own, fighting a lonely battle, asking herself what was right and wrong. Back at St. John's sin was in every book and prayer. It was the very warp and weft of their whole lives!

'Is there anything the matter, my dear?'

She caught a whiff of cologne. Not the stuff her father used! Was it right for a priest to be so worldly? Father Connolly pulled up his chair and put his hand on Rosie's knee. 'So you have been at St. John's Abbey for twenty years. Do you think in all that time you have come any closer to God?'

Rosie didn't know if she had. She had certainly been backing away from him in the last ten days. 'I hope so . . . '

'Twenty years is a long time. For you, the best years of your life. Twenty years ago I was only thirty-two years of age. I have been a priest for eighteen years and now,' he laughed, 'at fifty-two I don't suppose I'll ever get into the running for Pope!'

A middle-aged woman with dark features and silver hair came into the room with a jug of coffee. 'Thank you, Clara. This is Sister

Mary Rose, the nun I was telling you about. Sister Mary Rose, my housekeeper.'

She smiled at Rosie, put the coffee things down.

'I understand that you would prefer your mother to be buried rather than cremated. After all, we all come from the earth and it is, perhaps, a comforting thought that we may, if we so wish, return to the earth . . . '

At least he agreed with her. Rosie had always hated the thought of cremation — your whole body, once so vibrant and full of life being slid into some ghastly oven and burnt to an unrecognisable cinder barely a week after death. The cremation ovens were so final, so awful, and she had always believed that the living earth was a much more natural place to put down your bones for good.

'I have arranged for your mother to be laid to rest in a very pretty corner of our church yard. It's twelfth century . . . old and peaceful.'

Rosie thanked him. She had been worried about that, worried that there would not be room in such an old place of rest. He was very kind. Maybe she had been wrong about him. She wondered how long he had been in the parish and what his predecessor had been like. She remembered the young and handsome Father James, who had been close to her family and guided her across that narrow, ill-lit threshold into the contemplative life all those years ago.

Rosie noticed the way in which Father Connolly studied her clothes. No doubt she should be wearing her nun's habit. Wanting to break an awkward silence, she described how she had been sent to Medjugorje to report on the happenings there.

'Medjugorje? Where on earth is that?'

Rosie found it difficult to believe that he had not even heard of the place, when over ten million people had already been there. 'It is a village in Yugoslavia. Six young children saw the Virgin Mary there about ten years ago and they have been seeing her ever since. She comes with messages about peace, prayer and conversion.'

'The Virgin Mary is supposed to have been seen in many places,' Father Connolly said dryly, 'mostly by superstitious peasants in practically third world countries. Why doesn't she show herself in the teeming cities of the western world? Surely she has a message for them, too!'

'It may be that the peasants are more receptive, because their minds are not clogged up with the lust for power and wealth,' Rosie countered. 'Anyway, when I was in Medjugorje I saw hundreds of people, many of them rich Americans who had spent large sums of money to travel all the way to Yugoslavia, because they had heard about those visionaries and they wanted to see what was going on. Isn't it a revelation that, though she appears to the poor, hundreds of thousands of wealthy people from all over the world either believe, or want to believe, that what is happening there is true?'

'I would like to hear more about your trip to Medjugorje. We could arrange for you to come and speak in church about it.'

Rosie felt the colour in her cheeks. She wished he wouldn't keep touching her. She stood up, 'I must go now. I have to see the solicitor — to sort out my mother's affairs.' She blushed as she made for the door. She had just told a deliberate lie to, of all people, a priest. And once outside she began to wonder how many more lies she would have to tell in order to live an ordinary decent life in the outside world.

★   ★   ★

Rosie spent the next few days sorting out her mother's things, tidying up the house and answering letters, while Bill went to work in the garden. The neighbours kept an ominous silence, and nobody called at the little house.

Were they ostracized already, Rosie wondered, suspected of living in sin? Wasn't anybody capable of thinking of anything other than that time worn and incredibly ugly subject of sex? Her mother had died. Was there no compassion for her in the village?

The dreaded day of her mother's funeral came at last. She wore the same black lace dress, wide-brimmed black hat and veil that her mother had worn at her father's funeral.

★ ★ ★

Bill felt an ungainly bulk alongside her — strangely out of place — as they walked up the aisle together. The packed little church bore testimony to the love and esteem held by the villagers for her mother. As he entered a great silence descended on the crowded church and Bill was uneasy. He suspected that they thought he was after all he could get from her mother's estate. After all, isn't that what most people in the outside world felt about things? Gain — what was in it for them. He thought of what they would think if they discovered that he was a monk, and tripped on the flagstones.

They sat in the front row, Bill looking for all the world like some clumsy best man. The flower-covered coffin was set down beside them. He could see that Rosie was trying not to look at it. From what he had been told, this had been the most wonderful person in the world, loving and full of life. And here she lay dead, beside her devoted daughter who could almost reach out and touch the well-polished wood.

The blooms seemed to float in his tears. It had been the custom at St. Joseph's for one of the brothers to conduct the burial service over a dead colleague and Bill knew the words by heart. The monks had often preferred to be buried at sea, and for Bill, the service in the little church brought memories of rough waters, a tossing boat and the coffin sliding into the water. Bill was pleased that Father Connolly put feeling into his words, and spoke so warmly of how she was loved by all who knew her, for her care for those in need and the happiness she spread around her. Bill glanced at Rosie. She looked like a dream, standing there so slim and lovely in all that black lace. He hoped she gained comfort from the sincerity with which the parish priest had delivered his words of remembrance.

★　★　★

Rosie sat down to read her letters of condolence. Instead of bringing her cheer, they renewed her feeling of sadness. There was also a letter from the convent at St. John's Abbey: 'We deeply regret the loss of your mother with whom we hope you will one day be reunited in heaven . . . ' She did not know quite how to interpret it. She was not at all sure they understood her feelings . . .

A knock interrupted her thoughts, and Father Connolly put his head round the open door. 'I thought I ought to have a word with you in private,' he guided her into the kitchen and closed the door behind him so that Bill could not hear anything. 'It is just that you will be aware of the gossip in the village . . . ' There was an intensity in his face, which she hadn't seen before. 'You have been through a terrible time, my dear, and because you will soon have to return to the convent I was wondering about your mother's things. I suppose you are not allowed any possessions at St. John's, and you will be called back into the Abbey in a very short time. Would you like me to find good homes for her possessions — amongst the less well off in the village?'

Rosie was stunned. Her mother had just died. The Will had not even been read and she had dozens of problems to handle. How could she possibly dispose of everything? The idea of giving away all her mother's property seemed almost indecent, and for the first time a doubt began to stir inside her. Was it really a bad thing to have money and property? Her mother had had all that and if anybody deserved to go to heaven she did. So what was it all about? Had she been right in giving up twenty years of her life for God when she could have reached him anyway? 'I would like to talk to Mr. Oldham before I make any decisions.'

'Ah yes, I must speak to you . . . This Mr. Oldham. I don't want to be personal, but do you mind telling me who he is and how you came to meet him? As your parish priest you will understand that I am responsible for your well-being and . . . certain things.'

'What sort of things?'

'Look, let me be frank. You belong to the convent at St. John's Abbey, which is a very old order. I know them well. It must have occurred to you that to go around with this man who, I believe, is no relation, is simply not the done thing for a nun. And the Reverend Mother would be very upset if she heard about it on the grapevine.'

Rosie wanted to tell him that it was simply not done for a priest to interfere with her mother's private affairs so soon after her death, but she had been brought up to fear and revere all of God's representatives on earth. 'I shall tell the Reverend Mother everything, as I have always done, when I return to the convent. I have nothing to hide.'

'I'm sure. It is your innocence that makes you so vulnerable . . . ' Father Connolly smiled and shook his head. 'Look, you really should break off your relationship with this man.'

'Bill will be going back to work again very soon, then you . . . the village will have nothing more to gossip about!'

'What does he do?'

'I really don't know.' Another lie!

'You don't know? Why, he could be anybody, a criminal on the run, a trafficker in drugs, anything. Does he know you are a nun?'

Rosie hesitated, flustered suddenly, not knowing whether she should tell another lie. 'I don't know. I may have told him. What does it matter?'

The priest put his hands on her shoulders. How dare he! He was treating her as if she were a naughty child. 'What does it matter? Don't you know that some men have a thing about nuns? A nun represents . . . purity . . . you know what I mean!'

Rosie didn't. She had never had any

occasion to think about it. All she had been told over the past twenty years was to treat everybody as if he or she were Jesus. What sort of a world then was it out here? Was it some kind of purgatory people had to go through? Again she longed to be back behind the comparatively comfortable walls of St. John's Abbey.

'There's nothing wrong with Bill. He's a good clean open-air farming type.'

'Oh, he's a farmer.'

There. Again! 'If you'll excuse me. I have a lot of letters to reply to . . . '

* * *

Rosie continued to sort out her mother's clothing, books and other possessions, 'I'm going to have a big bonfire, Bill, and get rid of a lot of this stuff. The rest I'll take to the jumble sale.'

'You do what you think best. I'll leave you to it.'

But as she held the old familiar things she knew in her heart that it would be impossible: almost like parting with her mother for a second time. Without further ado, most of the clothes were put back on their coat hangers, and she hardly threw anything away. The house would have to be sold and everything would have to go, but . . . She decided to put it all off until another day.

When Bill came back from the village everything was neat and tidy again. 'I don't see any bonfires out there!'

'I just couldn't do it. They were so much a part of her.'

'One advantage of being at an Abbey — we have nothing to leave. It can't be easy to throw away things that belonged to someone who remains so deeply loved. God has blessed you with an incomparable mother and he asks you now to let her return to Him in total thanksgiving . . . '

Rosie was grateful. Bill was kind; he had depth and she would miss him when their time came to part. She needed him more than anybody, and the thought of him going off to some remote island off the coast of Scotland while she went back to St. John's, and the fact that they would never see each other again, made her feel sad and helpless.

★ ★ ★

In the days that followed Rosie had many callers, dressed up in their best clothes and bearing flowers. Most of them were genuinely sorry that Rosie's mother, whom they had

93

known for so long, had died. There were those, too, who knew that Rosie would soon have to return to the convent, and wanted to be first on the scene when the house and its contents were sold. If a nun were to sell her property there were sure to be bargains. Why, the rumour went around, if she were a real nun she would probably give everything away.

As Rosie came out of the kitchen she noticed a small group of people, notebooks in hand, peering into the rooms. They were busily jotting down whatever took their fancy. The local estate agent, John Reynolds, was there, too. 'Let me know when you are ready to put the property on the market. The house is situated in a wonderful position with lovely views across to the mountains. It would make an ideal holiday home for some of those wealthy people in London. I am sure we can get you a good price,' and he named a figure, which staggered Rosie.

The next person to arrive was Mr. Perks, her mother's solicitor, a well-built broad-featured man with wide-awake eyes. 'There are some papers I would like you to sign. Probate, income tax, you know the sort of thing. And I will need your national insurance number. I am sure you understand.'

Rosie did not understand. She had never had anything to do with income tax or national insurance, and she doubted whether her name was in any of the official records. Come to think of it, those twenty years in the convent had made her into a non-person, an outsider among her fellow creatures, and, if the truth be known, she had no allegiance to anybody, Queen or country. 'I don't think I have ever had a national insurance number and I am sure that I have had nothing to do with income tax.'

Mr Perks, a serious man, was taken aback. 'Everybody had something to do with *that!* Yet, come to think of it you have a point. A nun doesn't have any money or possessions . . . ' He frowned. 'How shall I fill in the appropriate forms . . . ? Will the Inspector of Taxes swallow it all?' Then a smile crept across his grey, wrinkled face, 'There will be taxes to pay, there always are, and then there will be the estate agent's commission and my own fees . . . '

Rosie was tired of all this talk about selling. First the local priest, then the estate agent and now the solicitor. Suppose she didn't want to sell anything. She could keep the house and let it out to some nice people, perhaps a clergy family, when she returned to the convent. That would serve them all right! And then she remembered she was not allowed to have any possessions.

Why shouldn't she live out her life like her mother? Had she been carried away by all that youthful idealism so long ago? Could she now, somehow, be freed from her vows? Again, that bogey, excommunication, hovered like a sword of Damocles above her, and she pulled herself up, feeling ashamed. How difficult it was to stop the devil from entering her mind!

⋆ ⋆ ⋆

One evening when Bill was out Father Connolly called on Rosie and invited her to a small party in the village. Apparently somebody had felt sorry for her, and wanted to try and cheer her up. They had also discovered that she was a nun, and were interested to meet her. Rosie, taken by surprise, could hardly refuse. She left a note for Bill and accompanied Father Connolly to one of the smarter houses in the village.

The party was in full swing with loud music, drinks and dancing. Most of the people there were young, the girls dressed in brightly coloured trendy outfits and, to her mind, very little on top. Rosie wore a plain cotton skirt and blouse. Even without make-up she was an attractive woman, but she looked decidedly out of place in that noisy room. Rosie tried to hang back, Father Connolly gently pushed her further into the room. Almost as if their entrance had been a signal, the heavy music stopped and Rosie stood there, nervous in the bright lights, while Father Connolly introduced her to one of the small groups. 'This is Peter and Angela, Dotty and, ah yes, Auntie Bell. Sister Mary Rose is a nun.'

Rosie began to feel even more uncomfortable. Just Rosie would have sounded better in a place like this.

'St. John's is an enclosed order and Sister Mary Rose has received special permission to attend her mother's funeral.'

Silence, Rosie could feel sympathetic eyes upon her.

'I don't think I've ever met a real nun,' Peter was the first to speak. 'All we want now is a full blown bishop and we'll be well away!'

Peter was a pale skinny-looking youth, whose nervous eyes made him an uncomfortable companion. Angela wore a colourful skirt, which dragged on the floor and gave her a bohemian appearance. Her hair was bound in a soft cotton fabric, and it so demanded Rosie's attention that she didn't notice if the girl was pretty or not. Dotty, with her auburn hair and bright hazel eyes, looked nice, but she was quite unable to stop talking. Auntie

Bell, known as 'Auntie' to almost everybody in the village, was fat and jolly and she, too, liked to chatter all the time.

In the next room the music started up again, most of the crowd started clapping and singing. Some were so excited they were jumping up and down, and skipping about. Rosie had seen nothing like this in her life. What devilish debauchery was this? How could Father Connolly of all people bring her to such a place?

Then to her utter amazement the music changed to something resembling a gentle love song, some fell to their knees and others lay prostrate on the floor with tears streaming down their faces. What had she got herself into?

The music calmed her and she recognised the name of Jesus! It was a love song to Him! People were holding their arms up to heaven and calling out His name. There must have been a lot of people there from other countries as the singing that followed was not in any language she had heard before. Eventually after some lengthy prayers the room went quiet. Father Connolly and his companion were welcomed in, and Rosie's own smile was wide and spontaneous. These people were so radiant; their happiness was contagious. Not for them the sober life behind confining walls of an Abbey, they had found a joy beyond her imagination in the normal world . . . and all in the name of Jesus!

★ ★ ★

Bill had gone to bed and Rosie, fearful that he would wake up, crept up to her room. That night, for the first time ever, she forgot to say her prayers. She dreamt that she was back at St. John's. She'd had a row with the Reverend Mother and decided to leave the convent, but it was night time and all the gates were closed and locked. She managed to climb over the wall only to discover that the entire population of the village were standing there, watching her. She managed to get back across the wall, but . . .

A large hand was shaking her gently, 'Rosie, Rosie, wake up. You were calling out in your sleep.'

'Oh, Bill, it was an awful nightmare.'

'It's all over now, come downstairs. I'll make us a nice cup of tea.'

7

The long hot summer drew on into harvest time and Bill and Rosie offered to join the volunteers from the village. 'I have always thought that harvest time must be fun,' Bill enthused. As they strode up the road to join the other workers they could hear the old Welsh songs. 'I remember reading that in the old days a man with a scythe could reap an acre a day. Imagine keeping that up day after day. I reckon he would have needed a pretty hefty breakfast, probably washed down by huge quantities of the farmer's cider. A bit like putting fuel into an engine . . . and with the back-breaking work it would have paid dividends!'

Bill had the time of his life pitching balls up to the women on the top of the trailers and when one of the tractor drivers asked him to take over while he had a break he was like a boy with a new toy.

'Do be careful, Bill, are you going to be safe driving up and down those slopes?'

'Don't worry, Rosie, it doesn't look that difficult, I'll take it steady,'

Rosie was working on top of the trailer,

pulling and shoving the bails into a regular two layer pattern so the finished load would be stable enough to ride the steep winding lanes back to the barn.

It had been a long hard day and that evening, sitting down to a late supper, they enjoyed the companionship of the villagers. The weather had been kind, and the harvest was safely gathered in. Everyone was happy at the end of a good day's work, not least of all the farmer whose wife had laid on a massive spread in gratitude for the voluntary help so cheerfully given. Someone produced a harmonica and another joined in the song. Then Rosie broke the spell, 'Only two more weeks and we will both be leaving all this.'

Bill looked sad, too. 'And goodbye to all this freedom.'

'Do you think we shall ever see each other again?'

Bill shook his head. 'Frankly, no. This seems to be our one big chance to see something of the world, and whatever there is out here, there is always hope . . . '

'When I go back all this will seem like some strange dream.' Rosie twisted her fingers around each other. 'We are all so busy at St. John's, perhaps we don't give enough thought to what goes on outside. Although we do have all sorts of people in from the village, as well as visitors from the other religious orders. Then there are the school parties and open days, and we have a programme of retreats throughout the year. We have no television, but the Reverend Mother has a radio and she keeps in touch with world events on behalf of us all. I don't suppose anybody can visit your place easily, stuck out there in the Atlantic?'

'As a matter of fact we have just completed a helicopter pad so top people, visiting clergy and the like, can come across without feeling thoroughly seasick. Then there are the boating enthusiasts, who pride themselves on making the journey. The landing can be difficult, because the sea is always rough. The fishing boats come across with supplies of freshly caught fish and sometimes we show people over the monastery and give them a meal.

'A television documentary was once made about St. Joseph's and we had writers with their cameras all over the place. So one way and another people seem to know we're there and we really are kept quite busy. That big stretch of water is always a deterrent, though, and we believe that the monastery will still be there long after the rest of the world has blown itself up or died of Aids!'

Rosie looked into her lap. 'Would you still

go into a monastery if you had your time over again?'

'I have been thinking about that. Life is certainly restricted, but mixing with people, sharing their trials and tribulations and earning a living is difficult and often fraught with danger. Life out here is like travelling down a rough, dark road, without a signpost or a lamp to show the way around the potholes.'

'If we could ask Jesus, what do you think he would say?'

'Probably, 'Go out into the world and preach the gospel!''

'What a pity we can't stay on here for a little longer,' Rosie sighed. 'I have been away a long time, but this is still my real home.'

Bill smiled, 'I shall always remember you when I am back on that rock of mine.'

'Your island sounds such a wild and lovely place.'

'It is most of the time. We get all the Atlantic weather head on, but on the rare days when it is calm it is really beautiful. The island has always been a holy place, a natural fortress. Not even the Vikings could take it! I suppose your Abbey is a kind of fortress, too, and must have seen some turbulent times over nine hundred years.'

'As far as I know the nuns never actually

took up arms,' Rosie laughed, 'though the Prioress once addressed the troops before they left for Agincourt. We have a transcript of her speech in the Abbey library and it is much more rousing than anything Henry the Fifth ever said!'

★　★　★

Father Connolly had a restless night and he was feeling a little uneasy the next day. It was the day for the Confessional. He found it difficult to concentrate; he couldn't get Rosie and that friend of hers out of his mind. If only he could think of a way to send him packing. Then to add to his consternation a deputation of men and women came to his house with incredible news: 'Bill Oldham's a monk!'

David Evans stepped forward. 'It is true, Father. I was working in the fields and I found this medallion!'

He showed the priest a bronze cross, which bore the inscription 'Brother William Oldham, St. Joseph's Abbey'.

When the full meaning of this sank in Father Connolly was even more disturbed. The villagers were in an angry mood and Father Connolly was unable to calm them down. He tried in vain to plead with them, but they would not listen. Should he telephone the police or just hope those excitable Welshmen would cool down?

★ ★ ★

Rosie was standing at the sink when a brick smashed through her kitchen window. Shocked and terrified, she stared at a broken plate. Angry hate-filled faces filled the window — like something out of a bad dream.

Bill had heard the noise and rushed to her side. 'What's going on? Stay here. I will go and find out what that gang of louts is up to!'

'We won't have you two living together in our village,' one of the men shouted. 'We'll give you twenty-four hours to get out!'

So that was it. Bill struggled to control himself, he was visibly capable of fighting back if the odds were more even. He tried to tell the villagers how he had met Rosie under entirely innocent circumstances in Yugoslavia. It only brought a yell of derision. 'I know it sounds ridiculous,' Bill continued. 'When Rosie lost her mother I came to help her and when her affairs are settled she will go back to her Abbey and I will go back to mine.'

This brought more jeers and angry shouts. 'Tell that to the Marines. Do you think we were born yesterday?' The crowd moved

105

closer to the cottage and Bill ran to bolt the kitchen door. If they wanted a fight he was ready for it and he picked up a poker from the fireplace.

'What's it like with a nun?' somebody shouted. The laughter that followed had a dampening effect and they hesitated to rush the house.

'We're just good friends,' Bill said. 'We have done nothing wrong.'

'You have both brought shame on a good Welsh village!' A woman waved her fist. 'We will not tolerate it. If you want to do that sort of thing then go back to England!'

'Get out today or we'll burn your house down!'

At that moment a speeding police car arrived and the gathering was ordered to disperse. 'Maybe we should take you both in for safe custody,' the constable suggested. Bill and Rosie declined. Their last visit to a police station was enough, and they had no intention of repeating the experience.

Bill answered all the policeman's questions. The young man, who had never been out of the valleys, wondered what all the fuss was about. He waited until the villagers had departed and drove off to make his report.

The next day no milk was left on Rosie's doorstep; and when Bill went shopping for food nobody in the village would serve him.

'Talk about sanctions,' he said to Rosie. 'They'd starve us out if they could!'

'Let's try the next village. We can do all our shopping there.' The bus wouldn't stop for them and to make matters worse it started to rain.

'We'll go to that little grocery and post office shop on the edge of the village,' Rosie said. 'My mother used to write to me about a Mrs. MacBride who runs it. Apparently she is quite a character and I am sure she would help us.'

Mrs MacBride, a stout, middle-aged jolly type of woman, had already heard about Bill and Rosie in the village, but she had a mind of her own. 'I'll make a nice cup of tea while you sort out your groceries.'

'Such hospitality in this faraway land!' exclaimed Bill, 'But then you are Scottish!'

'I knew your mother. She was an old friend and a good customer of mine,' she told Rosie.

'They want to kick us out of the village,' Bill said. 'What do you think we should do?'

'What you are both doing is a little unusual. You should try and understand these people,' Mrs. MacBride said. 'Most of them go to chapel and they like to think they are very upright and religious. On the other hand you have just lost your mother and Mr.

Oldham can hardly camp out in a field, so I see no harm in what you are doing.'

'What do you think my mother would want us to do?'

'I can't imagine her telling you to throw Mr. Oldham out just when you need all the help you can get,' Mrs. MacBride reasoned. 'And after all, a nun should have a chaperone in this wicked world, and what could possibly be better than a monk who looks strong enough to take on ten men at a time!'

Sunday Mass was a challenge and Bill and Rosie decided to attend. Rosie wanted to sit at the back of the church where she would not be under the direct gaze of Father Connolly, and people would not be able to stare; and they could make a quick exit after the service. But it was Harvest Festival and the church was packed and all the seats at the back were full.

Bill and Rosie braved a sea of hostile faces until Mrs. MacBride, in one of the front rows, beckoned to them — indicating that there were some empty seats near her. They found themselves just below the pulpit and when Father Connolly mounted the steps to give his sermon he was able to look straight down at them. Bill and Rosie went up for the Sacrament and for one heart-stopping moment she thought that the priest would pass her by. She tried to walk slowly and with dignity back to her place, the way she had been taught at St. John's. They sang 'Plough the Fields and Scatter' and then it was all over, and Father Connolly hurried round to the front door to shake hands with everybody.

★ ★ ★

There was still a great deal to do before the solicitors could wind up her mother's affairs and Rosie managed to obtain a further fortnight's leave of absence. After all, what was another two weeks when Mother Superior would soon have her rebellious nun back for good!

Mrs. MacBride called at Rosie's house with some letters, holding up one in particular. 'As you are the representative of St. John's here in Treriver, I thought you would like me to give you this one first.'

Rosie glanced at the envelope. 'But it is addressed to the Reverend Mother at St. John's. I can't open her post.'

Mrs. MacBride held out the missive to Rosie who just stared at it. 'Well, aren't you going to open it?'

'But I have no idea who it is from or what it would be about!'

'I have,' Mrs. MacBride smiled mischievously at Bill, who had just come into the room. 'I know that writing better than anybody else's in this village!'

Rosie still hesitated. It seemed almost a sacrilege to open a letter addressed to the Reverend Mother!

'Somebody's written to the Reverend Mother at St. John's and Mrs. MacBride thinks I ought to open it,' Rosie told Bill.

'Whose writing is it?'

'Di Evans's,' Mrs. MacBride said. 'He's a real Holy Jo. This spidery scrawl of his seems to haunt my little post office! He is always writing to this place and that causing trouble for some poor soul.'

'Here, let me do it.' Bill took the envelope and ripped it open. 'Dear Reverend Mother. As a good Christian, I feel that it is my duty to report the following matter. Sister Mary Rose, as you probably know, is staying in her family home in order to conclude her late mother's affairs in this village.

However, it has come to my knowledge that, while in Yugoslavia on a mission for your good self, Sister Mary Rose became acquainted with a Brother of some ancient order. They came back to England together and I regret to have to inform you that they are at present living together, in her house.

110

Since Sister Mary Rose is quite brazenly ignoring the wishes of the decent people of this village who want them both to leave this place, I feel that I must write to you. I hope that, with both our prayers, she may yet receive forgiveness and salvation. Yours most respectfully, David Evans, Esq.'

When the occasion warrants, a good round cuss makes any man feel better, and Bill, from whose lips Rosie had never heard a swear word or curse, swore now. The two ladies looked startled.

'And if David Evans is a 'good Christian' as he claims . . . then I'm not so much a monk as a monkey!'

This brought a laugh from Mrs. MacBride while Rosie, saddened by the contents of the letter, sank into a chair and wondered whether she should go back to St. John's at all. Why should she humbly confess her sins to the Reverend Mother when there would never be any real forgiveness?

★　★　★

A letter from Rosie's solicitors contained more heartening news. Apart from the value of the house her mother had left her the substantial sum of £100,000. 'They say that the house could sell for as much as

111

£200,000,' she told Bill.

But Bill was looking a little glum. She guessed what was on his mind.

'I'd have to give it all away, yes, I know, and the Reverend Mother would expect me to give it all to St. John's!'

She knew, too, that even if it were a million pounds it would never be enough to wash out the stain in that letter. But the Reverend Mother had not seen the letter yet. It lay there still, on the kitchen table. Rosie said a quick prayer, snatched up the letter and tore it into shreds. She had been saved by Mrs. MacBride.

'Let's go away from here. Somewhere where we can both think. I would love to see your island. Would you take me there, just for a few days, before I have to go back? Just so that I can picture you living there when I am back at the convent.'

Bill was enthusiastic. 'What a wonderful idea. A few breaths of that Atlantic air and you'll feel like a new woman. Why it's worth going all that way just to listen to the thunder of the ocean in the caverns, deep beneath our monastery. Out there the sea seems to come up from the other side of the world to batter that old rock, but I reckon it'll still be there when everything else has gone!'

And then his face fell. 'Come to think of it

I don't believe a nun has ever been to St. Joseph's. Maybe nuns are not allowed.'

'But we have visiting male clergy all the time at St. John's,' Rosie said. 'Our entire order would collapse overnight if we tried to turn them away. Besides, Jesus's disciples were not all men!'

Bill was reassured. 'Of course it will be all right. The whole history of monasticism is based on welcoming strangers into their gates. More so I would say for nuns. There is only one snag — money! It's a long train journey to Scotland and then there's a good four hour boat trip.'

'That's no problem,' Rosie waved a letter in the air. 'The solicitors have released some money from my mother's estate so that I can handle affairs and pay the bills, and I would be very happy to pay for the return trip.'

Bill gave a laugh. 'Return trip? Once they got me back there they'd never let me go again!'

'You could say that you wanted to escort me back to the convent. After all, they would expect me to have a chaperone of some sort.'

'It's worth a go,' Bill grinned. 'We'll make history and land a nun on that bastion of male chauvinism. One last adventure together before we're both shut away for good!'

Bill and Rosie told Mrs. MacBride that

they would be going up to Scotland for a few days.

'Rosie would like to see St. Joseph's so I thought we'd go up there together while we have the chance. The trip will do us both good and perhaps the village will calm down a little while we are away.'

★ ★ ★

They made their arrangements and set off for the railway station a few days later. The little branch line station was crowded and one of the first men they saw standing there was Di Evans, waiting to meet somebody off the train. It was impossible to avoid him and he believed, quite naturally, that the Reverend Mother had received his letter and had ordered Rosie back to the convent. Bill Oldham, too, was leaving at last. Ah well, at least he had done his duty.

His moment of triumph then turned to misgiving. If Rosie was leaving then any chance of persuading her to sell the cottage to him cheaply was leaving with her. Maybe in writing to the Reverend Mother he had overplayed his hand and with something like panic in his heart he hurried to greet her. 'I do hope you are not leaving us so soon!'

Bill, remembering the letter, was not in the

mood to mince words. 'You'd sell your own grandmother if you had the chance!'

Bill's voice carried and the people standing around stopped and stared.

'What on earth do you mean?'

'You wrote to the Reverend Mother at St. John's.'

Di took a step back and Bill had never seen a man look so surprised. 'That letter was confidential,' he stuttered.

Rosie, not wanting to be seen in a slanging match in public, went on ahead, while Bill looked as if he was about to hit the obnoxious little man. 'How could you write such things about a completely innocent young woman. You ought to be ashamed of yourself!'

He caught up with Rosie leaving an angry and bewildered Mr. Evans standing there. How could the Reverend Mother, of all people, possibly disclose the contents of such a private and confidential letter?

'He thinks he's got rid of us,' Bill said as the train came in. 'I can't wait to see his face when we get back!'

★   ★   ★

All Rosie could remember were the old steam trains and the rather shabby railway stations. Now, the trains were sleek and comfortable

115

and they hurtled along at breakneck speed while the railway stations seemed to be in competition with each other for the most elegant flower display. When they arrived at the little fishing port of Bellsea, Bill and Rosie decided to change into their habits for the last lap of their journey to St. Joseph's.

When she rejoined him she was no longer the woman he had met in Yugoslavia and with whom he had shared so many exciting days. She was Sister Mary Rose; he swallowed hard, somehow, she was more inaccessible than ever.

The skipper of the fishing boat offered to take them across to the island of Toy and as they headed out to sea Rosie reflected, 'You never told me what you did before you went to St. Joseph's?'

'I was the manager on a small farm in Shropshire.'

She had been right. He was a farming type; at least, before he became a monk!

'Were you ever married?'

Bill shook his head, 'No, I was engaged for a while.'

Rosie waited, hoping he would tell her more . . .

'Her name was Sarah . . . She worked in the city, and always wanted to go to the Lake District — in Cumbria.'

'Was she pretty?'

Bill looked out across the water to the horizon where the clouds were heaped up like some new mountain range in the sky. 'She was slim, blonde, like many career girls in London,' Bill paused. 'Have you ever seen a gentian? Her eyes were that same blue. She was beautiful . . . '

'What happened? You sound as though you loved her a lot.'

'We went on holiday to the Lakes. She was fascinated with the place. One day we went for a picnic. We parked the car close to one of those mountains not far from Keswick. We had a lovely quiet lunch together. Then she said she would like to climb the rocks. I told her it would be impossible without the right equipment. But she knew I didn't like heights and thought I was making excuses. She teased me for being a wimp.'

'What you? Never!'

Bill shrugged, 'After the picnic I went down to wash the dishes in a stream and when I got back Sarah had vanished. She had gone ahead with the climb, and had got well up the side of that mountain. I could see her up there, clinging to the rock face. She was standing on a tiny ledge of rock and she was in real trouble. She just didn't understand how the thought of heights like that had always given me the willies. But I couldn't just stand there. I knew she couldn't hold on for long, and if I went to get help she would fall off before anyone arrived. I shall never know how I managed it, but I climbed up until I was just above her. She was scared and blue with cold. I clung to an overhanging rock and grabbed her hand, but the climb up had taken all the strength out of the muscles in my arms and I couldn't pull her up. She was right. I was a wimp. I couldn't hold her. I hung on to her for what seemed forever, but as our hands went numb she slipped through my fingers, and she fell to her death.'

Rosie shook her head sadly. 'Is that why you went to St. Joseph's?'

'I suppose so. Partly. It all added up. The sad thing is that now I have done so much outside work with primitive tools I would probably have the strength to save someone.'

Rosie placed her hand over his and together they watched the rolling seas, each lost in their own thoughts.

8

The island of Toy protruded like a mailed fist out of the sea, and from it rose the sheer walls of the monastery: it was easy to understand why the island had been chosen as a bastion for Christianity. This chunk of rock was all that was left of the old world. Beyond lay the Great Sea, once believed to spill over the very edge of the earth.

As they crossed from the mainland Bill's mind was in turmoil. Was this place where he should spend the rest of his days on earth? 'I wasn't happy here before I went to Yugoslavia and now I have fallen . . . ' At this moment all he could do was to hope.

Bill tried to put a brave face on it, laughing at the gulls as they screeched and reeled around the tossing boat. 'Look, Rosie! We are coming into the quay. And there is the Abbott running down the quayside! He always makes a point of welcoming the fishermen personally.'

Bill stepped out of the boat and proffered his hand to help Rosie out of the boat. The wind caught her billowing gown, emphasising her slim figure and pretty features; he could not suppress an appreciative grin.

'Thank you, Bill. The Abbott doesn't look very happy.'

That, thought Bill, was an understatement. The Abbott was furious! He could not disguise his displeasure; all his usually spontaneous hospitality for visitors completely erased, his anxiety in seeing a woman on his island utterly transparent!

Bill attempted a formal introduction. 'This is Sister Mary Rose from St. John's Abbey at Rockensand.'

The Abbot greeted Rosie briefly and took Bill aside. 'Who on earth is this? No female has ever been allowed on the island of Toy, let alone one from a convent! Thank goodness I came down to the quayside in time to prevent her from entering the monastery itself!' He paced up and down for a moment or two. 'Didn't you think what you were doing?'

Bill had thought about it, but he had dismissed it as ridiculous. Things like that just didn't make sense in this modern age. Surely a nun, a holy woman, who belonged to one of the oldest orders, should be welcome today in any monastery. He told the Abbot their tale, 'And Rosie wanted to come across to St. Joseph's, because she is particularly interested in old . . . '

'Rosie!' The Abbot looked at Bill. 'That trip

seems to have turned your head!' And for a dreadful moment he wondered whether one of his Brothers had taken advantage of his brief spell of freedom and fallen into sin. The sooner he heard this man's confession and he could start over again with a clean slate the better! 'She is not allowed into St. Joseph's. No nun has ever set foot inside this monastery!'

'Surely in this day and age . . . '

'Not in any age!' The Abbot pointed to where the fishermen were unloading their crates. 'Sister Mary Rose must leave the island immediately!'

'She can't leave now. It's a four hour crossing and it'll be dark when she gets in.'

'I am sorry.'

'But she's a Christian, dedicated like all of us. We can't just turn her away like that! How could we turn anyone away?'

'And we cannot change our rule, suddenly, after eight hundred years for any woman. If we put this matter to the vote none of us here would want her to enter the building.'

'Nonsense! We are talking about the faith here, not superstition! Sister Mary Rose has been a nun for twenty years. She has been a student of history and would very much like to look over the monastery. Afterwards, I will take her safely back to St. John's.'

The Abbot shook is head. 'You will do no such thing!'

'She would be alone on the quayside over there.'

'You have been away from us quite long enough. I must ask you to remain here.'

Bill tried to reason with the Abbot, 'And there are no trains until morning.'

'Sister Mary Rose will have to return to St. John's on her own.'

'Surely all my years with you here have earned me the small favour of escorting this nun safely back to her Abbey? I would be back here again the day after tomorrow.'

'I cannot allow one of my brothers to spend the night with a nun on some Scottish quayside, or anywhere else. Quite clearly your time away from us has upset you.' It was cold standing about on the quay, the Abbot shivered. 'You must choose. If you stay here with us now all will be forgiven, but if you leave with Sister Mary Rose you cannot return to this island!'

Bill tried to explain all this to Rosie and she shook her head in disbelief. 'But we have visiting male clergy . . . '

The Abbot shrugged and spread out his hands. 'I am sorry, but I am speaking not only for myself, but our whole Brotherhood here. If you were to stay the night I would be creating a precedent and I would then have to open my doors to all and sundry.'

Rosie was shocked. 'I see now how the church regards women!'

The fishermen had finished their unloading and were ready to cast off. Rosie went and took her place in the boat. 'Goodbye Bill, I shall pray for you.'

Bill looked up at the building, which had been his home for ten years. If he were to go now he would lose everything and whatever he did he would lose Rosie. Yet how could he live with a rule that forbade a nun of all people from seeking shelter in a Christian monastery? Bill didn't know what to do . . . until the fishing boat's engine started up and the vessel began to move away from the little pier. He could see Rosie's upturned face, pale and smiling, yet sad, and he knew then that she was about to go out of his life forever. The Abbot was saying something to him, but he broke away and ran across the quayside and jumped down into the boat. 'Rosie!'

★ ★ ★

The crew had never seen a monk and a nun kiss each other before and neither had the Abbot. The fishermen were silent and a little awed by their two passengers. They couldn't wait to get back to the mainland to tell their story, if it wasn't good enough for a few free beers, nothing was!

⋆　⋆　⋆

The sun sank slowly into the sea behind them as the fishing boat headed towards the mainland. Bill stared at his fast-disappearing, island home and wondered about the future. There would be no job, no home . . . and Rosie? Something about the dark swirling water beneath him only seemed to add to his despair.

'It's all my fault,' Rosie took his hand. 'If I hadn't persuaded you to take me across to St. Joseph's you would have been allowed to stay on there.'

'I am glad you did,' Bill looked down into her anxious face. 'I never realised how narrow my life was. Besides, I was thinking of leaving anyway, which was one of the reasons why I took up the offer to go abroad.'

'Cheer up. We'll spend that last week walking and exploring the Welsh hills together, and when I am back at the convent you can always come and see me on open days.'

'Open days?' Bill muttered gloomily. 'Once

or twice a year? I don't even know if I'll have a job let alone be able to afford the fare to Rockensand!'

'What about the family farm. Surely they could use a strong man like you?'

'I don't know . . . my parents are tenants. I can't see the landlord letting me take over . . . '

★   ★   ★

Rosie had been thinking about that, too, and decided that before she went back to the convent she would see that Bill had enough money to keep him going until he got a job. And she would not be in any hurry to give all her legacy away to charity. The Reverend Mother would expect to receive a substantial proportion for the upkeep and general maintenance of St. John's Abbey, but Rosie decided to postpone any further decisions.

It was dark when they went ashore at Bellsea and the next train to Glasgow was at seven a.m. the following morning. They still had a little money left and decided to stay at The Last Hope, which was the village's only inn. Nightlife in the little dockside pub was in full swing and they had to push their way through the crowded room to the reception desk.

The rough dockside workers and fishermen were not used to seeing monks and nuns in their pub and everybody stared. 'Where's the fancy dress party?' was the most pleasant jibe they received.

'Hey, that's a new slant. Monks and nuns! And I thought we'd had 'em all!'

'We are looking for two single rooms for the night,' Bill informed the landlady. 'We've just come over from the monastery and we've missed the last train to Glasgow.'

The landlady looked surprised and a little suspicious. Her thoughts were clear to any observer: monks and nuns were the last individuals she would expect to see in her pub. 'You have come across from the monastery?' She tried to catch them out. 'Who is in charge over there now?'

'Father Dominic is still there. He has been the Abbot of St. Joseph's for twenty years.'

She ran her finger down the register, determined not to take any chances. 'I can put you in number three,' she handed Bill a key, 'It's just along the passage.' He, at any rate, was likely to be genuine, because there was a monastery out there across the water.

She looked at Rosie more carefully. She had never seen a nun in Bellsea, let alone in her hotel. Monks she could understand because men got up to all sorts of tricks.

Nuns? Well, she believed that a woman's place was in the home, cooking the Sunday roast and bringing up the kids. Anybody who shut themselves away for life in some grim institution must be distinctly odd! 'I can offer you number twenty-six in the annexe. It's over there, on the other side of the building.'

When Bill and Rosie came down to supper dressed in civilian clothes the other customers were disappointed. It was not often they could have a good giggle about a monk and a nun. They looked like anyone else in ordinary clothes; it seemed to take the zing out of the situation.

Rosie chose a corner table that looked out across the darkened harbour. 'You should go back to the monastery. I cannot have it on my conscience . . . Listen, tell the Abbot that I will make a contribution towards the upkeep of his monastery if he will forget everything and have you back.'

'Bribery?' Bill smiled. 'Unless the Abbot can have me back as I am, without a penny, and unless he can forgive me my sins, I would rather be cast out into this terrible world to make peace with my Maker in my own way. And if the Abbot cannot do this then there is more truth and beauty in a single flower on that old rock than anything they are trying to do there!'

'He would, he said he would . . . It was because of me that you are in this situation. I should not have come. It was stupid and childish to ever think that your Abbey would allow me inside.'

Rosie picked up the menu and tried to hide her tears. Bill was the first real friend she had ever had and she was soon going to lose him. Surely this friendship was a gift from God? How could she now say goodbye to him forever? She remembered her vows. She had sworn to surrender everything to God. Everything. And that would certainly mean any ongoing friendship with Bill.

★ ★ ★

Word had gone round the village that a monk was staying at The Last Hope inn, and the local people, mostly sailors and fishermen, merely shrugged and smiled. Hardly anybody, except the fishermen, had actually been to the monastery. As far as the villagers were concerned the monks of St. Joseph's were an unapproachable lot, a kind of holy club, which did nothing to encourage membership. News that the monk had a nun as a companion, and at their pub, gave the whole place food for gossip.

'Pity they're not staying longer,' was the

landlord's opinion, 'give business a boost!'

'I heard she wasn't allowed ashore over there . . . ' one of the customers started.

'It's true, the old Abbot chucked her off — her being a woman and all that!'

'I always said women should know their place.'

'You're right there!'

Bill and Rosie moved from their table to have coffee in the lounge. Immediately the talking died down and they knew they were the objects of curiosity. Religion inspires varying degrees of awe. Clergymen are seen to be different to ordinary folk. And monks and nuns are more different still. It was only a matter of time before someone summoned up the courage to come across and talk to them.

★   ★   ★

A reporter from the local newspaper was the first. He wanted a story. Something about life in monasteries, particularly St. Joseph's: the island was fairly close and yet he had never been there. 'Could you tell us how long the monks have been there and why they don't come and see us here in Bellsea?'

Bill tried to explain that monks shut themselves away in monasteries in order to lead a life of contemplation and prayer. 'They

129

believe that only by complete isolation can they best serve the rest of humanity.'

'Why don't they come out into the world and see life in all its stark reality? Seems to me they are trying to escape from all that!'

'There are churches and cathedrals and a whole army of clergy to take care of the outside world,' Bill suggested. 'The fact remains, the people of the world owe their entire Christian faith to the small number of monks and nuns who kept it going for hundreds of years in far away places like St. Joseph's. People like that stood out against the barbarian hordes of Europe, and it was only possible to do this by finding some lonely island and building a fortress there for their home. Monks and monasteries have their place in this world, as do bishops and cathedrals. Nuns, too, seem to be able to hold their own in this cruel world of male chauvinism. Both have picked up the fallen standards of our hopes and prayers and carried them high to this very day!'

Bill, in his enthusiasm, began to wonder whether he really should throw this lifestyle away. Should he not go back to St. Joseph's on the very next boat and plead for the Abbot's forgiveness? And yet, how could he leave Rosie to travel all the way back to Wales alone? He wanted to be sure that she would be happy, with all her affairs sorted out, and above all he wanted to be sure that Father Connolly and those Welsh villagers were not going to gang up on her. And if there was ever a hope . . .

The reporter broke in on his thoughts. 'If I were a monk I would be worried about shutting myself away from the rest of humanity in some far flung monastery for the rest of my life. Sounds like escapism to me!'

He asked whether it was true that Rosie had been refused permission to remain on the island and Bill explained what had happened. 'She was not allowed to stay. No woman has ever been allowed inside that monastery. It's just one of their rules.'

The reporter was scribbling away and Bill guessed that he would exaggerate his story out of all proportion to the facts, and he could only hope that the national press would not get hold of it.

'Why don't you stay on for a while and look around? The west coast here is beautiful.'

'I'm afraid our time is running out and Sister Mary Rose here will have to return to her convent.'

'And you will have to go back to St. Joseph's?'

Bill shook his head. 'No. I've left. I've resigned.'

By the look of deep concentration on the reporter's face, Bill realised the young man could see the potential for a scoop. He thought about it from a journalist's viewpoint. Pretty nun and a sacked monk together. The reporter wanted them to change back into their monastery clothes so he could take their photograph, but Bill refused and, despite his protests, the man stepped back with his camera and took a picture of them sitting there at the table. Bill began to wonder, uneasily, what the outcome of all this would be and he was glad that he and Rosie wouldn't be around when the paper came out.

9

They caught the first train out of Bellsea the next day and arrived back in Wales late that evening. The following day they called at Mrs. MacBride's little shop for some provisions.

'Back already? Was the sea too rough for the crossing?'

'The Abbot wouldn't let Rosie stay. That place is strictly for men only!'

'That's religion for you!' Mrs. McBride was shocked. 'And you, are you going back yourself?'

'No. They're still living in the ninth century. It's not for me!'

'What will you do?'

'I'll be all right. I've learnt a few trades over the years: carpentry, electrical work, painting and decorating, gardening, that sort of thing. I like this part of the country and I'll probably stay on here and try and get a job.'

When Mrs. McBride was silent he said: 'I know what you are thinking. After all the rumpus nobody will take me on. Well, it's a challenge and I don't scare easily!'

Mrs. McBride pulled out a couple of daily newspapers. 'This'll scare you!'

Bill and Rosie stared unbelievingly at the headlines: Abbey Throws Nun Out! Monk And Nun Spend Night Together In Pub!

Rosie picked up one of the newspapers, the one that the Reverend Mother always read: Monk And Nun In Love — Together!

And there was the photograph, the one that the reporter had taken of them both in the hotel dining room. Rosie began to feel quite faint.

'Why don't you sit down, my dear?' Mrs. McBride's voice seemed to come from far away. 'It's only the newspapers. Everybody knows they print a pack of lies.'

★   ★   ★

The next day Rosie said she had been awake all night. 'It was the thought of going back and leaving you here alone . . . '

'I'll miss you; I'll be lonely, too. Ten years in a monastery like St. Joseph's can put you into shape for anything except loneliness. Let's keep in touch and I will come and see you on every possible occasion.'

Rosie knew that he was saying that to comfort her. Visitors were hardly ever allowed except on open days or if you were sick or dying!

It was Sunday and she decided to wear her

nun's habit to church. 'I suppose you could say it is a kind of penance.'

'A good idea,' Bill agreed, 'and I will wear my cassock and we will both lend a little dignity to this so-called Christian village.'

'But, Bill, are you allowed to now? I suppose if you are still considering the idea of going back, it's all right. I am sure the Abbott would forgive you . . . '

'I'll wear it today. I know I must make a final decision. In truth I think is very unlikely that I will ever go back.'

The church was almost full, but they managed to find two seats right at the back. Bill realised, too late, that it was not such a good place after all; they would still have to face the entire congregation on their way back from taking the Sacrament. The service ended and Bill and Rosie, anxious to beat everyone to the church door, were the first to leave.

'It's a lovely day. Let's go for a walk. I'll show you my favourite place,' Rosie said. 'When I used to live here a girl could walk for miles across the countryside and return home in the dark in perfect safety.' She led him across a field of wildflowers until they came across a lane, which ended in a cornfield. A track led steeply up into thick woods and petered out. They passed only one person, a farm labourer, who stopped and stared at the two figures who might have stepped out of the pages of history.

They came out of the wood and Rosie tried to get her bearings, but dense thickets now covered the hillside and the path she remembered was completely overgrown. She sat down on a log while Bill began to kick around in the long grass.

'Look, there's an old railway line!'

'Of course!' Rosie exclaimed. 'There were old slate trains running up here. I used to lie awake at night and listen to them. Sometimes I could see the sparks from my bedroom window. There was a slate quarry up here in these hills, but it has been closed for at least twenty-five years.'

Bill went on ahead, kicking away more turf, exposing more of the narrow gauge track.

'The track used to come all the way up from Pen, almost eight miles away.'

Bill tried to picture the little engines puffing their way across the rugged countryside. Red, green and gold with gleaming pistons, and a long line of trucks, each brim full with slate for the nation's roofs, trailing out behind. As he followed the track, which sometimes disappeared into dense thickets, he could see the slate that had fallen off the trains and local people had missed.

'Wait for me!' Rosie called.

Bill stopped and grinned back at her. 'Let's follow this line and see where it goes!'

'My brother and I used to come up here to watch the busy little trains. We'd wave to the driver and his mate who'd wave back to us.'

The railway line was rusty, but not twisted or warped, and the heavy, old, creosoted sleepers seemed to be as good as ever. As they excitedly uncovered more track it was as if they had stumbled upon some archaeological find. The rails led straight on through the woods and, though the trees were close, none of the roots seemed to have disturbed the line itself.

Bill ran on, remembering how, as a boy, he would pretend to be a train. Rosie had to run hard to keep up with him. They came to a set of points where a branch line curved off into the trees, Bill stopped and pointed. 'Let's see where this one goes to!'

They followed the line, trampling down the bracken, the discarded fragments of slate cracking beneath their feet, and Bill pictured the mine, somewhere up above them, the caves long abandoned now, and probably inhabited by bats. They came to a dilapidated railway shed, and a line of rusty trucks standing in a siding.

Everything looked run down and neglected.

'Looks as if nothing's been used since the quarry was shut down. I don't suppose anybody has been up here for years!' There were no doors to the shed, and Bill called, 'There's a large piece of rolling stock inside. It's a brake van!'

'What does it do?'

'They used to have one coupled on the end of a line of trucks, like a guard's van, so that if anything went wrong the man inside could throw on the brakes. Very necessary, too, on these gradients!'

The front of the van was fitted with an outside platform so the operator could signal freely and see what was going on, and it was here, too, that the controls were situated.

'It's what they used to call a gravity track,' Bill enthused. 'I have read about a lot of things while I was on Toy, and I once came across something on the Welsh gravity trains. In those days they had to use horses to pull the empty slate trucks back up to the quarry, and when all the trucks were loaded again they simply rolled down the mountainside under the force of their own weight. The line was laid out on a very gradual slope all the way down. All the same a fully loaded slate train was something to reckon with, because its momentum was tremendous and if an emergency stop was required they sometimes had to allow as much as a mile's notice, and if the brakes didn't work the whole train would become a bomb!'

'I'd hardly call that an 'emergency' stop, Bill!'

'You're right!'

Bill explained, 'With the coming of locomotives in the 1860's, the gravity line could operate much more efficiently; there would be no time wasted resting and changing the horses on the long journey up to the quarry.' As they stood there admiring the brake van they looked at each other, sharing the same thought.

Rosie smiled. 'Let's!' They climbed up onto the open platform, after examining the controls, Bill eased off the brake lever to see if the van would still roll, but the mechanism had seized up with rust and disuse. He searched the shed and found a heavy hammer and gave it a blow. Another blow. The van gave a lurch. And before he could do anything to stop it, clanking and screeching in protest the heavy vehicle moved slowly out of the shed.

Ahead, the track was overgrown with grass and barely visible. He could just see a set of points and he tried to apply the brake, but nothing happened. They both held their breath as the van clanked and squealed its way across the points on to the other line where a thick old shrub arrested the van's progress. 'Thank heavens we weren't going any faster!' Bill said anxiously. 'Once that thing got moving there would be no stopping her.'

Bill climbed down and proffered his hand, 'Help me down, Bill.' As Rosie pulled her gown about her to jump down from the platform they heard a series of snapping noises as the brittle wood gave way . . . 'Quick! It's moving again . . . ' They watched helplessly as steadily, the van picked up speed.

'Jump, Rosie, JUMP!' He caught her as she dropped.

The heavy brake van with its big steel wheels clung firmly to the rails and crushed everything in its path. It was out in the open, accelerating wildly. And when the steady clanking of the wheels changed to a more disturbing clatter Bill's mind began to race, too. 'Rosie, what have I done? How could I leave the van to run away? I should have stayed on board.'

'What could you have done? The brake wasn't working. You couldn't have stopped it!'

'I could have shouted a warning or something . . . ' Bill knew he sounded ridiculous.

'We were both acting like a couple of kids. All we can do is to get down there as soon as we can. There isn't a 'phone for miles.' As they scrambled down the hillside they could see the van hurtling its way into the distance, getting smaller and quieter the further away it got. 'It has to go over a gorge. There was a nasty accident there years ago. I dread to think what condition the bridge is in now. Pray, Bill, it's all we can do.'

'Oh, God, what have we done!'

★　★　★

The easier gradient had ended and the line had begun its long sweeping descent to the valley below. The swaying and jolting van seemed to cut through the undergrowth like a knife. Would the bridge, long in disuse, take the weight? There was no water down there, just a wilderness of rock. Bill put his arms round Rosie and together they shuddered as they heard the violent vibrations of wheels on track as the ancient vehicle rattled its way down to the valley below. Out of their sight now, it passed one old signal box and another, and a dilapidated railway station. An embankment began to build up on both sides; on it thundered, still accelerating the van picked up even more speed in the tunnel, and was now running through one of the built-up areas close to the railhead at Pen, slipping past the old working-class houses, roads, shops and railway sheds . . . The van clattered towards yet another signal box at a country halt. Alerted by the horrendous noise, with lightning reactions the signalman grabbed his cloth and wrenched the lever to throw the points ahead of the errant beast.

The platform at Pen was crowded with Sunday trippers and holidaymakers, climbing aboard the Swansea train. Passengers turned this way and that, 'What's that racket?'

One woman screamed, 'It's going to crash into us!'

'No! It's on the narrow track,' the porters cried.

At last the track started to rise and the heavy brake van's velocity gradually dropped until it clattered alongside the town's High Street. Several small boys ran alongside, trying to keep up with the best entertainment in their young memories. The narrow gauge track ended in a dingy part of town alongside some sheds and old rolling stock. By now the van was only travelling a few miles per hour, even so the impact on the buffers rang out like an exploding cannon shell.

'Wow! That was a brilliant stunt!'

'Must be for an advert of something!'

'Wonder what for!'

'I bet they didn't plan on it going out of control like that!'

'I bet they did!'

'Where are the cameras then?'

'Yea! You've got a point there!'

⋆　⋆　⋆

By the time Rosie and Bill arrived, shaken and bruised, in Pen the commotion had died down, and the enthralled spectators were none the wiser that they had been the cause of all the excitement. Engrossed in their stories they did not take much notice of the bedraggled gowned characters in their midst. But the runaway train would be the subject of casual gossip for weeks to come.

'Thank goodness no-one was hurt.'

'That old thing must have been up in those hills for years. I wonder what made it take off like that?'

'It can't have just got going on its own . . .'

⋆　⋆　⋆

They took a bus back to the village and Bill enthused about the little trains. He told Rosie about his passion for steam trains and how much, as a boy, he had wanted to ride on the footplate; the driver and his mate; the big glow from the fire; eggs fried on a shovel and the mugs of tea — there would always have been plenty of hot water! A whole life on the footplate, and the yarns exchanged between the driver and his mate would have filled a book or two!

'What a waste; a perfectly good track. They used to build them well in those days!'

'What do you mean? What a waste?'

'All you need is one of those little slate pulling engines,' Bill said, 'and you're in business. I'm surprised nobody's thought of it before.'

'You mean fun rides. Narrow gauge rails and all that?'

'Right. They seem to be very popular in Wales, especially where there used to be slate mines or collieries. This one is just waiting to be opened up for holidaymakers and steam train enthusiasts, not to mention the kids!'

'But, Bill, it has been closed for such a long time. I don't think anybody would consider buying it in its present condition.'

'The track is as good and solid as ever and we have even put that bridge to the test. One of these days somebody with a little money will buy a couple of old engines, do them up and have a go. As for the carriages . . . you remember those old trucks sitting back there in that siding? All you need to do is fix some seating in them and you're in business — in a small way to start, of course. And from the money you make during the summer you could improve the system and buy better stuff for the following season. Mind you, the bridge would have to be looked at. The whole track would have to be examined, but if a heavy old brake van can make it all that way down to the town it says a lot!'

The bus dropped them about a mile from Treriver before continuing on its way along the main road. 'Can't say I've seen the likes of them in my bus before,' the driver remarked.

'It's a sign of the times, you never know what you'll see these days!'

And the other passengers agreed.

★   ★   ★

Rosie laughed nervously. After a day when her emotions had run the full gamut from childish excitement to fear of the consequences of their mischief, she was glad to be back home in one piece. 'I wonder what the Reverend Mother would have said!'

★   ★   ★

Two days later Rosie received another letter from the Reverend Mother. She had dropped her usual dictatorial style and adopted a more conciliatory tone in her efforts to win Rosie back. 'I was distressed to read about your association with Brother William Oldham in the paper the other day, and I was shocked to see your photograph in that paper. I have managed to keep all this to myself, but I am afraid the Bishop and the other clergy are sure to see it eventually. You will understand that this sort of thing does not do the ancient name of St. John's any good at all, and it is perfectly clear to me that the devil has entered into both you and this man, and I urge you to pray with what strength you have left and ask God to save your soul from being lost forever. Come back, my child. Leave this William Oldham and the wicked world. Come back to us here where 'you will not fear the terror of the night, nor the destruction that wastes at noonday . . . ' Above all remember your vows!

The Reverend Mother'

Bill saw the look of despair on Rosie's face. 'Bad news?'

She handed him the letter.

'You don't have to go back,' Bill said when he had read it. 'They could make life pretty awful for you. This sort of thing makes me

146

glad I'm out of it all!'

'Does that mean you have made a decision about Toy?'

'Yes.' He read the letter again. 'So she thinks the devil has entered into me.' He smiled at Rosie, 'What do you think? After all, he comes in many disguises!'

Rosie gave a wan smile. 'No devil could find a place in you, Bill! She's right though. I should remember my vows and it really does all come down to that!'

'I swore an oath, too.'

'Yes, but it was the Abbot who caused you to leave, not you.'

Rosie lay awake that night. She didn't want to go back to that bare, convent existence, but neither did Jesus want to die on the cross! She remembered part of her vow: 'Will you for the rest of your life, and forsaking all else, devote your whole mind, body and soul to Almighty God that he may transform you into the likeness of Christ?'

And as she tossed and turned, she remembered the railway and how, as a child, she would lie awake in this very same room and listen to the trains at night. A rumble like thunder would have her hurrying across to the window to watch the glow from the footplate, the sparks shooting up into the night as the little slate train came chugging through a cutting in the hill.

Bill loved the railway, too. Suppose she sold the house and gave him enough money to start a narrow gauge railway business. That would provide him with work. Or would it be wrong to deprive the Abbey of an endowment? If she were to help Bill like that would it be stealing money from God? And yet, if she returned to the convent for a life of prayer would not that put it right with her Maker? She decided to go back to the convent and beg the Reverend Mother's forgiveness. She would carry her cross just as Jesus had to carry His!

When Rosie came down for breakfast she told Bill that she had decided to keep her promise to God and go back to the convent. 'As for the money, the Abbey is so richly endowed I would rather give most of it to you. I would like to give you the chance to start your very own business, and I know how much you love trains!'

Bill was overwhelmed. 'It would be a dream come true! I can't tell you how grateful I am that you thought of doing this for me, but there would be some big snags.'

He tried to thank Rosie, but she could tell that he was pessimistic. 'I know there will be problems. We've got to find out if the owner will sell first, and also whether we can buy an engine and all that, but I'll soon have some money and it's worth looking into!'

It was possible. Other railways had done it and there would be no competition, their nearest competitor was over fifty miles away. All they had to do was find the present owners and take it from there.

'Let's do it today,' Rosie was keen to see that everything was in order before she left. 'It's nice to daydream, but let's go into Pen and see what we can find out.'

'I'd much rather we went into this together. Do we really have to split up? Do you really have to go back to St. John's Abbey?'

'I am afraid so. I don't think I could live with myself if I broke my vows. But we are allowed letters, so we can keep in touch and you can tell me how things are going on!'

'I'd write to you a lot. I'd send you photographs, too. I'd call it Rosie's Railway!'

She laughed and shook her head. 'The Pen Railway sounds much better!'

'Promise me that if you ever change your mind you will come in with me, so we can run this venture together.'

'All right, but it rather looks as if I'll be a sleeping partner. But first let's see if the whole thing is possible!'

★　★　★

In Pen they made their way down to the old railway sheds and disused buildings. Most of the glass in the office windows had been smashed and the place was strewn with litter. It was difficult to imagine that this had once been the centre of a busy slate mining business. They were picking their way through the debris when Bill saw the name Thomas & Co. in peeling red letters on one of the buildings. They went to the Town Hall and the local Chamber of Commerce and discovered that a Thomas family had owned the quarry since 1850, when the railway had been built and slate mining had started in earnest. The title to the narrow gauge railway in Pen belonged to the last surviving member of that family, a Mrs. Thomas, aged ninety-eight who resided in a nursing home just outside the town.

'So far so good,' Rosie was in a hurry. 'Let's telephone them and go along and see her as soon as possible.'

10

The nursing home was situated on high ground overlooking the little railway, which was probably why the owner of that railway had decided to spend her last days there. A nurse pointed out a pretty old lady with snow-white hair and the deepest of blue eyes. 'There she is.' She raised her voice slightly, 'Mrs. Thomas you have visitors.'

'That's nice!' The elderly lady held her hand out to Rosie and smiled, 'Come and sit down here, my dear.' Bill followed and stood behind Rosie's chair.

'What a well mannered young man you have! Now tell me why I deserve this honour.'

Between the two of them, Bill and Rosie told their tale. The old lady's eyes lit up at this unexpected intervention in the dull routine of her nursing home life. She had previously been an active and successful businesswoman, but since entering the nursing home she had found life tame. 'So you two were the cause of the runaway van! Well I never! And to think I am the only one who knows. How exciting. I could have sworn I heard some rolling stock go by the other day

151

and I thought perhaps I had been dreaming.

She went across to the window and stared at the scrub-ridden, overgrown track. 'I had similar ideas myself once. It's not going to be so easy. You would have to get planning permission for a start. And that bridge would not pass a safety inspection. The previous bridge collapsed about seventy years ago with loss of life and a whole trainload of slate went into the gorge. The new bridge was supposed to be absolutely safe, but people said it moved a little when a train went over.'

'But isn't that natural in a structure of that nature?' Bill asked hopefully.

'I don't know. You will need to consult a civil engineer. At the time nobody made much fuss about it. Apart from the odd railway worker, those trucks were only used for carrying slate, and the old hands were used to it. That bridge had always been a problem and a subject for local gossip. It was one of the reasons why we had to close everything down in the end.'

Bill's enthusiasm began to wane. It would be decidedly risky to run a whole train across the gorge, and building a new bridge across that gap would cost a fortune!

'My grandfather built that railway on a very gradual slope all the way down to the valley,' Mrs. Thomas continued. 'After all, a fully loaded slate train was an enormous weight and with the town at the bottom he had to be sure there would be no accidents!'

Bill and Rosie looked at each other sadly. 'There's a lot to think about.' Bill said.

'There certainly is!' Rosie agreed, but in a more determined voice. She was not going to be discouraged . . . yet! 'Could you possibly consider selling?'

'I would, but I am afraid you would be the loser. You have to cross that bridge before you can run all the way down to Pen. What would you do with miles of useless railway line?' Mrs. Thomas looked down wistfully at the track beneath her window.

Mrs. Thomas told them that her grandfather bought the land to build the railway from the various landowners, mainly farmers. It was fairly easy in those days, because they would have hardly noticed the loss of such small strips of land, and the railways would have benefited them; they could use the empty trucks to bring up goods and machinery to their farms. The railway line and all existing rolling stock, including the two old locomotives, belonged to her. 'I very nearly sold the lot for scrap a few years ago, but I changed my mind. I couldn't bear to see it all broken up with cutting apparatus and sledgehammers, especially those two engines.

They were such old friends.'

'Where are the engines now?'

'Puffing Billy and Panting Bess? They are still down there in one of the old sheds. Trouble is, every time we put new glass in the shed windows they get smashed by hooligans. One of these days they'll break in and climb over everything . . . but they won't be able to do the engines much damage, they really built things to last in those days!'

Bill asked, 'Why didn't you sell them to a museum?'

She just shook her head. 'Never! As long as I am alive Puffing Billy and Panting Bess will stay safe and sound just down the road from here!'

'Unless we can bring them back to life,' Bill said, 'and then you can see them chugging away past your window!'

'Oh, wouldn't that be wonderful! Just to see all those happy children. It is my dream to see Puffing Billy and Panting Bess working again!'

If it wasn't for that bridge, Bill told himself bitterly. If only they could find out exactly what condition it was in and whether it would be possible to strengthen the foundations in some way. Building a completely new bridge would be out of the question.

'We would like to see the local surveyor, as

well as consult an engineer, about the bridge — and the entire track. If we receive a satisfactory report and the bridge could be strengthened in some way, and if the railway line were safe, we would like to make you an offer for the whole property.'

Mrs Thomas gazed at the rusty and weed-ridden railway line in the distance. 'If only you could bring all that back to life! Yes, do what you can. I know the Borough Surveyor quite well, a Mr. Jones. Here, I'll write down his address. The engineer who used to look after the railway is a Mr. Davies and he is still in business here. He will have all the particulars about the railway including the bridge.' She gave them the address of both men. 'This will be something to go on with and I do wish you both the best of luck!'

'May we look at those two engines?' Bill asked.

'Of course. Mr. Davies has the key to the shed and I am sure he will be very pleased to give it to you. Give old Puffing Billy and Panting Bess my love, won't you?'

Davies & Co. was a busy little firm of engineers. The walls of the reception room were covered with pictures of the various engineering projects that had been completed in the district, and there were the usual impressive-looking framed certificates.

Mr. Davies, an elderly-looking Welshman, took them into his office and after introducing Rosie, Bill told him about their interest in the railway. 'Mrs. Thomas suggested we see you. She, of course, would like to see the railway reopened and we were wondering whether you could advise us about the safety side of it all.'

'Safety side?'

'Would there be any problem for a narrow gauge railway business? For carrying passengers . . . The bridge, for instance?'

'You are not the first people who have thought of opening up a narrow gauge railway business here,' Mr. Davies said. 'After all, it's a natural when you think of what is going on in the rest of the country.'

He pulled out a file and thumbed through some papers. 'There have been some quite well known people interested in the past and either they've been put off by the bridge or Mrs. Thomas didn't like them. How much money have you got?'

'I could probably raise about £200,000 from the sale of my house,' Rosie estimated, 'and I would like to put £100,000 into the venture. I shall be going away myself for some time, and Mr. Oldham will be running the whole thing. The other £100,000 would go into buying a cottage for Mr. Oldham. If any more is needed I am sure my bank would give me a loan against the security of the railway and part of the takings.'

Mr. Davies laughed. '£100,000 wouldn't go anywhere. There's those two engines, some carriages of some sort, a ticket office to be set up, signal equipment and the whole railway line would have to be checked, and last, but not least, that bridge would have to be made absolutely safe!'

'Mrs. Thomas told us about that. Do you think it could be made safe without having to build a new one?'

'The Thomas people were always having a go at repairing it. They refused to acknowledge there was anything much wrong with it. The cost of a new one would have put their slate quarry out of business. Nowadays everything has to be properly examined and passed by safety experts. It's something to do with one of the bridge supports having weakened at some time or another. The layer of rock it's driven into is probably too thin in the first place. Anyway, they tried to shore it up with concrete, but nobody had the sense to dig down and see just how deep that rock went!'

'Do you think it is necessary to build a completely new bridge?' Bill asked.

'No. Why, today you would be talking

about a million pounds, and that's what's been putting everybody else off from buying this railway. The bridge is there. All the rest of that structure is fine.'

The engineer lit a cigarette and inhaled deeply. Bill wondered when all the smoke would stop coming out of his mouth.

'I tested that bridge myself, once. Nothing official you understand. I don't like heights, but I had myself lowered down to the rocks at the bottom. I had arranged for an engine, complete with a string of loaded slate trucks, to cross the gorge. I was a bit scared, I don't mind telling you, when that old engine came chugging along. The support moved about a couple of inches and I felt like running, but the train passed over safely to the other side! I tested all three other corners of the bridge in the same way, and they were fine, so there is just that one side of the bridge to worry about. In my opinion, nothing a few tons of concrete won't cure.'

'What do you think it would cost?'

'I don't know. Not all that much. There's not a lot of work involved and the workmen can bring their transport right up to the bridge itself. All you'd have to pay for is the cutting out, etcetera. I suppose at a rough guess about £30,000.'

'What about the line itself, would that be safe enough?'

'I should think so. They used to put railway lines down to last forever in those days. The whole track would have to be looked at, and all the undergrowth cleared away, and that tunnel checked over.'

'Do you think the Borough Surveyor would pass the bridge as safe if we did what you suggest?'

'Can't say until a train has been over it and it has been thoroughly tested. It may be that you'd spend all that money on repairs and have it turned down flat. Anyway, I suggest you have a chat with the surveyor, Mr. Jones first.' Davies scribbled on a piece of paper. 'Here's his telephone number, and if you do decide to go ahead and take a gamble on the thing I will be very pleased to act as your engineer!'

Bill was a bit dubious, 'Could we borrow the keys to the shed and have a look at the two engines?'

Mr. Davies took down the keys. 'Sure. Here you go! By the way, those two engines are the best thing in this deal. They may look a bit dirty, but they're both in tip top condition and they are real collector's items!'

When they had gone Mr. Davies's secretary came into the room. 'Those two, sir. I saw them in church over at Treriver last Sunday!'

'What's wrong with that? Lots of people go to church.'

'They're that monk and the nun, sir. You know, the ones in the paper, and they were dressed up as a monk and a nun in the church, too.'

'Are you sure?'

'Yes, sir. I'll never forget those two.'

The engineer cursed. Come to think of it he remembered seeing that story, too, among all the other scurrilous reports on page three; he hadn't recognised them dressed in ordinary clothes. 'Looks like they're a couple of crooks masquerading as a monk and a nun whenever it suits them. How low can you get? They've probably emptied the church box already!' He swore when he remembered that he had lent them his keys.

'And now they're trying to get round poor old Mrs. Thomas! I'm off down to the engine shed and I've a good mind to telephone the police. People like that ought to be locked up!'

* * *

Bill unlocked the heavy padlock and swung the gates open. The two engines stood there side by side. 'They both looked as if they

160

would be more at home in some far flung country!' Bill mused, 'Although Britain used to make her own locomotives, we also imported special trains for mountain railways.' They climbed up on to the Puffing Billy's footplate.

'That one over there is Panting Bess,' Bill said. 'Aren't they beauties, just raring to go? Looks like the whole thing is going to cost too much, though. I bet you can't buy a couple of engines like that for less than £25,000 each and then there's all the rest of it!'

'No harm in finding out,' Rosie persisted. 'You never know, the old lady might let it all go for a song, because of that bridge.'

'But it's no use to us if the bridge is too expensive to repair.' Bill said.

'I don't know what you think, Bill. But I am not too happy with Mr. Davies. I don't know anything about engineering, but I didn't think he sounded too convincing . . . '

'Tell you what. If we get the Health and Safety people in we'll get a better idea, and their opinion is the one that matters.'

When they climbed down from the footplate they were confronted by Mr. Davies, who had entered the shed unobserved. 'Hey, you two, clear off, and if I catch you around here again I will call the police!'

Bill and Rosie stood there nervously. They

had never been spoken to like that before. 'I don't understand,' Bill said. 'You said we could look at the engines.'

'You're a couple of rogues!' the engineer exclaimed. 'Monks and nuns indeed! One minute you pretend to be in holy orders and the next you are trying to swindle a poor old lady. Don't think I haven't read about you two in the papers. Now give me back those keys and get the hell out of here!'

'But I am . . . was a monk,' Bill said, 'and Rosie . . . '

'Am? Was? What sort of rubbish is that! You two may go around fooling the rest of the country, but you don't fool me!'

'We have already explained everything to Mrs. Thomas and now I suppose we've got to go through it all again with you!' And so they repeated their tale . . . 'And you can look at Rosie's ring.'

Rosie showed him her beautifully inscribed ring. It had been placed upon her finger so devoutly following the saying of her final vows; the ring which bound her life and soul to Jesus Christ forever!

Mr. Davies, a Welshman, was not without sentiment and after looking at these means of identity he swallowed hard. After all, he could be wrong. Monks and nuns did funny things these days and come to think of it Mrs. Thomas was not the sort of person to be taken in easily!

Davies muttered an apology. 'Got to be careful. There are so many people pretending to be this and that, and I think that we in Treriver have grown to be suspicious of strangers. Only a week or two ago a man came into the estate agent's here and asked to be shown a house. Well, it turned out that he squatted there and refused to move out. As you know the law takes a long time, and he is still there, lighting fires in the grates, cooking for himself and living there at everybody else's expense. Apparently he had been hanging about in the Black Mountains. Pity he didn't stay there. But he speaks well. I'd call him a gentleman vagabond if there is such a thing!'

The Black Mountains? Thorndyke! It looked as if he had found this empty house more comfortable than camping out. 'We'll go along and talk to him and maybe we can do everybody a favour and get him out of there,' Bill said.

Mr. Davies's eyebrows shot up to his once hairline. Would these people never fail to amaze him!

★   ★   ★

When Mr. Davies had gone they called on the local Health and Safety Officer, and were surprised at how well he knew the railway. 'If you can fix that bridge so that it is a hundred per cent safe I'd say you were on to a good thing. Trouble is you'd have to buy the whole shooting match before any work on it could commence, and if it didn't pass the safety standard after all you'd lose the lot! The rolling stock needs to be looked at. Brakes can rust up after years of non-use. The track is as safe as the main line from Kings Cross to Edinburgh!'

'It's your money, Rosie. The decision has to be yours.' Bill insisted.

'Monks aren't trained in engineering.'

Rosie laughed. 'What about ex-monks!'

After twenty years of convent life she had been finding it much easier to laugh out here in the outside world and she had discovered that Bill, too, had a good sense of humour. Rosie giggled, 'Let's do it!'

Bill shook his head at her and smiled.

'Have you noticed how much easier it is to laugh in the outside world, Bill?'

'Indeed I have, and I am thinking that in many ways you are a lot happier, too.' Bill dared to hope that Rosie had become happier since they had first met on that far away hill in Yugoslavia. She acted in a much more natural and carefree way than when they first met. It was such a pity that she would soon be back again in the half-light of those austere walls. She needed to be out in the world, giving others the benefit of her sunny nature.

That evening Rosie wrote to the Reverend Mother. 'I've asked for another month's leave of absence. And told her there are problems over mother's Will — probate and all that — which is perfectly true. The solicitor said there would be many delays before any substantial amount of money could be released.'

Rosie read her letter through again, to see if she should make any changes. 'I think she will agree. She will be expecting a large part of the money for St. John's Abbey.'

'I would not want to upset you if I was in her shoes,' Bill said.

True enough; back came a letter granting Rosie a further four weeks, 'And that is the absolute limit. I am not prepared to seek special dispensation, and have no desire to explain your dubious actions to anyone.'

'We've got a whole month!' Rosie hugged herself with joy, 'Let's go and see if we can buy a railway!'

★   ★   ★

Mrs. Thomas pulled her chair closer to the window and stared down at the defunct railway. 'I expect they've told you the usual story: you'll have to build a new bridge!'

'Not really,' Bill said. 'Although it's not safe as it is. We would have to spend a lot of money on it to bring it up to the safety standards required by the authorities before we could carry holidaymakers.'

'I have been thinking about that. I will sell the railway to you for £30,000, rails, sheds, locomotives, lock stock and barrel, but you will have to bear the cost of the bridge repairs!'

Bill and Rosie were astonished. The two locomotives they had just seen were worth more than that, without the rest of the rolling stock and the track itself. The price was a giveaway!

'You are very kind,' Rosie said, 'but shouldn't you get professional advice? You would be letting us have it for a song!'

Mrs. Thomas shrugged, 'What does it matter at my age? What does anything matter? If I could sit here and watch the trains go by, especially if it brought happiness to children, I would practically give it all away. Unfortunately, I have one or two relatives who are expecting to get some money out of it. I'll ask my solicitors to draw up an agreement right away. In the meantime you can get your inspections done and get some estimates.'

★ ★ ★

On leaving the nursing home Rosie and Bill went in search of Thorndyke. He was no ordinary tramp. If they could persuade him to leave his squat the people in the village might be less hostile to all three of them.

They called at the little house Mr. Davies had mentioned, and after a long wait Thorndyke's bearded face appeared at an upstairs window. 'Piss off! There are at least a dozen empty houses in this village and all I'm doing is sheltering from the cold and rain and keeping the place warm for the owner. So clear off, because I'm just about to have my lunch!'

'Hey, don't you remember us?' Bill called up. 'We met you on the road a while back!'

The curtain dropped in to place, and heavy footsteps could be heard crossing the bare boards and thumping their way down the stairs. The front door opened and there stood their traveller friend, with a big grin creeping through a mass of unruly whiskers. 'Of course I remember you. Welcome to Thorndyke Lodge! Come in, come in and have some grub. I've got steak, eggs and chips on the go in the kitchen!' He looked at them suspiciously. 'How on earth did you know I was here? You're not ganging up with all the others to throw me out I hope?'

'Somebody told us that a tramp was squatting in one of the houses here, the description fitted, so we thought we'd come along and see if it was really you.'

'A tramp, eh? Is that what people are calling me now? How are the mighty fallen!'

'I thought you were going to winter it out in the Black Mountains. You mentioned a forester's hut.'

'I was turned out,' Thorndyke said, entering into the spirit of his tale. 'They would have roughed me up if I hadn't made a run for it. I found this empty house, but they've been trying to get me out. Talk about loving your neighbour. It's been worse than the Battle of Stalingrad!'

'How long are you going to stay here?'

'Just until the weather improves a little, but if they do get me out I can always shelter inside one of those old churches. They still leave the doors open around here, though there have been a number of thefts. Just imagine! Stealing from a church!' Thorndyke, ever the raconteur, recalled the time he had been locked inside a church all night . . . 'It was an eerie experience I can tell you! I'd had a long day on the road, and I was so exhausted I went into this old, Saxon church for a kip. The Rector or whoever came along and locked the place up without even bothering to take a good look around inside, and I was so fast asleep I didn't hear a thing. Not till I woke up to find everything was pitch black!'

'What do you mean? What did you hear?'

'People whispering and moving about.'

Bill and Rosie exchanged glances. 'Did you see anything?'

'I don't know. Imagination is a funny, very strong, thing. Spend a night in one of those old churches, with their ancient churchyards and those people buried there, all those characters, and you could believe anything by the end of it. I thought about something else while I was there, all the candles that get lit for one ceremony or another, or to remember someone. The warmth, the love . . . what happens to it all? I read somewhere that if you take a candle and blow it out the heat from that flame is never totally dissipated. There is always a warmth, however infinitesimal, which is still inside the universe because it cannot escape outside it!'

'I don't know about that.' Bill frowned. 'It doesn't sound like anything I learnt in Physics when I was a kid!'

'Pah! What do they know?' Thorndyke retorted.

'I never had you down as the poetic type. You've been spending too much time with your head in all those books of yours. What you need is a dose of reality. You told us you were in some kind of business, what was it you used to do?'

'Never mind all that. I'll tell you what I wouldn't mind doing again . . . '

'Go on then . . . '

'I used to love tinkering about with old cars. Really old ones — vintage stuff.'

After lunch, while Thorndyke did the washing up Bill took Rosie aside, 'Look, if we really get this railway thing going we shall need one or two people to help us out. If I'm going to drive the train we'll need a guard, for instance.'

'Thorndyke?' Rosie laughed.

'Well, yes. With that beard of his he's got the right looks. And he seems to be quite a cheerful sort of character — the kind of big uncle the kids would like. And from what he says he must be mechanically minded. He could be quite useful doing this and that.'

'Sounds a good idea,' Rosie agreed 'and he could have a room with us in the meantime. I am sure we could recruit local girls to do odd jobs — such as issuing the tickets and running the two stations.'

When they described their plans for buying the railway Thorndyke enthused, 'I've travelled around quite a bit — as you know — and I've seen those narrow gauge railways. Those old engines go on forever. Once you've got the thing going, and if you can keep your staff down to a minimum, it could be a money spinner!'

'Unfortunately, Rosie here will not be able to stay on with me.'

'Why on earth not? She'd be the main attraction!'

Bill steered him to a chair. 'It's a long story . . . '

Thorndyke sat in wide-eyed amazement hanging on Bill and Rosie's every word. 'Wow!'

'So you see,' Bill continued, 'Rosie would have to be a sleeping partner. She would keep in touch with developments. But what we do need is some extra help and we were wondering whether you would like to come in with us.'

Thorndyke laughed. 'Me in business with a monk and a nun! Now that's what you call an unholy alliance! What would you want me to do, teach Sunday school on the train?'

'If the whole thing goes through we thought your business and engineering skills might be useful, and you might like to have a shot at being the guard!'

'Me, a guard? You're joking!'

'If you do a good job we'll promote you to fireman and you can ride on the footplate with me!'

'Big boys with big toys, if you ask me!' Rosie lifted her chin and pursed her lips, suppressing a smile.

The two boys referred to put their arms around each other's shoulders, 'But we didn't ask you!'

'Aren't you two going a little too fast,' Rosie said. 'We haven't got over the problem of the inspection yet!'

Bill waved his arms about like an excited child, 'I'm sure the bridge can be strengthened. By the time we've finished it will take a dozen slate trains!'

In an effort to bring things back to some level of normality, Rosie looked Thorndyke straight in the face, 'You will have to leave this house.'

'What, go on the road, in this weather?'

'You can have a room with us providing you do some of the chores and make yourself useful!'

Thorndyke's countenance changed immediately. He grabbed Rosie and spun her round. Only too happy to leave his cold, draughty abode for a warmer place, he needed no second telling and had his meagre belongings packed up in no time, 'Lead the way, gorgeous!'

Bill laughed, pleased to see this destitute man so happy, 'Less of that!'

Word soon got around the village that not only had Bill and Rosie persuaded the tramp to leave, but they had also taken him in. The general opinion was, 'They can't be all that bad.'

★　★　★

Bill dreamt about trains and prayed that the whole venture would go through without too many hitches. Rosie wanted to set him up in business and make sure that he would be provided for. In his dreams she took a much more active role . . .

Rosie had asked for everything to be expedited. The examination of the bridge took place within days and the various reports quickly followed. The railway track and the tunnel were found to be perfectly safe. The bridge reinforcement was the main problem. The rolling stock was in need of some maintenance: wheels, axles . . . needed a good greasing up; the rest was purely cosmetic — de-rusting and bright coats of paint. When the house was sold, given the bank was still willing to lend them money, the whole thing was possible.

When the work on the bridge was finished it would be tested thoroughly, and there was no reason to think all would not go well, the project could go ahead.

11

A swiftly flowing stream ran through the little park in Treriver, splashing over the rocks and making a fairyland of rainbows in the sunshine. Bill had the bench to himself, and when somebody came up and spoke to him he tried to hide his irritation.

'Mind if I join you? You've got a pretty little island over here. I always thought that England was just concrete from one end to the other. When I started out from London this morning I couldn't believe all that countryside existed!'

Bill judged the man to be in his middle sixties, and very definitely American.

'My name's Shute. Wayne Shute.'

'Bill Oldham.'

'I've been looking round London. It's changed since I was last there many years ago.'

'Changed for the good?'

'Hell, you're kidding! Take your subway for instance. If you stand at the top of the moving staircase and look at the people coming up you'd want to up stakes and light out of there!'

'I know what you mean,' Bill agreed. 'I've been away for ten years and they frighten me, too!'

'London used to be great. Nowadays you might as well be in Johannesburg, Shanghai or Bangkok! You on vacation here in Wales?'

'I suppose you could say that, though it's more of a working holiday.'

'You're like me. I can hardly go anywhere without doing business of some sort. What's your line?'

Bill hesitated. How could he tell this businesslike American that he was an unemployed ex-monk? 'I am looking at railways, the narrow gauge type. There are some good opportunities over here in Wales.'

'For trips, joy rides, that sort of thing?'

'Yes. The old slate quarries have closed down, but the railway is still there and those old trains go on forever.' Bill was enthused and glad to have someone to talk to. He told his confidant about his plans for buying the railway. 'The old lady is going to let us have it for a giveaway price; the two engines, rolling stock, railway, the lot. Thirty thousand pounds would you believe?'

Shute listened attentively, 'Folk in the US of A are also bringing back some of the old railways for pleasure trips.'

'Most of the other Welsh narrow gauge

176

railways are up north. We should do well in Pen, because it's an easier route for the holidaymakers coming from London and Bristol. We'd be the first on the list as it were!'

The American shook hands with Bill and wished him luck, and when he had gone Bill felt a new excitement coursing through his veins, mingled with a feeling of importance. He was not just a humble monk any more, but a real businessman!

*   *   *

Bill and Rosie had arranged to see Mrs. Thomas the following week, to update her on the various inspections and tests. When they called the old lady seemed to be very upset. 'A very nice American man came to see me the other day. He offered me a hundred and fifty thousand dollars for everything and he said he would also finance a much needed wing here at the nursing home.'

Bill was furious. 'He wasn't called Shute by any chance, was he?'

Mrs. Thomas looked fearfully at Bill's grey face. 'As a matter of fact he was. Do you know him?'

Rosie had never seen Bill like this before. 'Bill! Whatever is it?'

They also discovered that Shute had

arranged to have a trial run in a couple of days' time.

The old lady was on the point of tears. 'How could I possibly refuse?'

'I quite understand,' Rosie took the woman's shaking hands in hers. 'I really can't blame you. Did you mention the bridge to him?'

'Oh yes, but he didn't seem to be worried about that. He told me that he had enough money to build ten new bridges!' She sighed. 'I wonder how on earth he came to hear about it. I would much rather have sold to you.'

Bill tried to choke back his anger and he cursed himself for being so simple and trusting. If only he had kept his mouth shut!

'Well, at least you'll be able to see the trains go by,' Rosie added comfortingly.

'There'll be trains all right,' Mrs. Thomas agreed. 'He told me that he was going to bring over one of those old western type steam trains. You know, with the cowcatcher in front and that mournful hoot!'

'A train like that wouldn't look right in the Welsh hillside,' Bill said, 'and that foghorn of a whistle, they'll be blowing that for the kids and it will drive everybody crazy!'

On their way back to the cottage Rosie tried to calm him down, 'Cheer up! You can stay on at the house and I am sure you will soon find a job.'

This was not what Bill wanted at all. 'But I won't have you, will I?'

★　★　★

Jack Evans had no appetite for breakfast. The whole village was talking about the way those people were going to team up with that tramp and take over the old railway and make their fortunes. He called to his wife, 'I'm just going to get something for the car.'

But he didn't go to the local garage. Too many questions would be asked. He drove into the neighbouring town where he was not known. 'Do you hire out oxyacetylene burners?'

'Have you used one before?' the mechanic asked.

Jack who was nicknamed Jack-of-all-trades, because he was generally a useful chap to have around, assured him that he had, 'I want the burner to free a drive shaft that's seized up on my car.'

'We need all our burners,' the man said. 'Can you do the job today and let us have it back first thing tomorrow?'

'No problem!' Jack took the apparatus back to his cottage and put it in the tool shed.

He said nothing to his wife, but by the look on her face he could tell that she suspected something.

'It's that monk and nun, isn't it? You shouldn't let them bother you. After all, what is to be will be and there is nothing we can do about it. If they decide to stay here and set up business it's up to them.'

As she turned to go back into the sanctuary of her kitchen, Jack muttered to himself, 'Oh yeah? We'll see!'

★   ★   ★

Jack listened for his wife's gentle snores, a sure sign that she was fast asleep, and took his torch and crept out to the shed. He stuffed the oxyacetylene burner into a large sturdy bag and set off across the fields in the direction of the railway. The night air was cool on his face, and a bright moon made the going fairly easy, though the equipment was heavy and cumbersome. His feelings were mixed: aggression and pride tinged with guilt . . . Why should he feel guilty? Was he not purifying the village? Getting rid of the devil himself from within their community? All the pent-up emotions of the last few months seemed to explode inside him and, as he staggered on through the darkness, he cursed and sweated until at last he saw the narrow gauge railway track, stretching out like some preposterous ladder through the trees.

Jack struggled along the track, fighting the undergrowth he tried to measure his stride to the sleeper spacing. It had seemed no distance when, as a young boy, he had been allowed to stand on the footplate. He realised all too well that it was one thing to cover the distance in a train, but quite another to attempt it on foot. With his heavy bag, Jack came at last to the shed where he had watched the men working years ago. It had all been rather fun, then. In the night everything was different. He went on, into the trees, following the railway line by the light of his torch, would he have enough time to do the job? At first he thought that distant whistle was a train, and he stopped again to get his breath.

Ahead, through the trees, the moon hung low like a barn lamp. He listened again, and then he knelt down and put his ear to the rail. Imagination, or was that a faint drumming as if, somewhere back there, a train was coming on fast? He was scared. He wanted to run off into the trees and hide. He wanted to forget the whole diabolical scheme. For Jack all this had become worse than a nightmare . . .

He stood and stared at the narrow gauge

181

track, undecided, and then he saw the dark skeletal outline of the bridge ahead and he was certain he had to do it!

He worked his way down the embankment until he found one of the steel supports. By torchlight he could not see any damage. Any weakness lay in the foundations. Jack paused. He was about to carry out an act of sabotage. In his own opinion, he had always been a righteous man; this was something entirely outside his normal way of thinking. But he must do it for the sake of the village, not for himself. He aimed the flame at the base of the support and as the sparks flew he cursed; he had forgotten to bring any goggles. He stopped to adjust the apparatus; the burner went out and he lost his torch. He scrabbled about in the pitch darkness, found the matches and relit the contrary contraption. He had only intended to weaken the support, so the movement of the bridge would be more pronounced when a train went across, and the safety inspectors would condemn it outright, but the flame was fierce and before long he had all but cut right through the metal.

He stopped. Fear eating into him. All his adult life he had been a religious man and now he was a criminal, possibly a murderer! He piled some rocks round the burnt and blasted end of the support and climbed back on to the railway line. He tried to run, but his feet were like lead. Every sleeper seemed to be a stepping-stone into eternity.

★   ★   ★

It was almost daylight when he arrived back home. The door was unlocked and he caught a glimpse of his face in the hall mirror. Gone were the features of the self-righteous churchman. The eyes, which stared back at him, were not his own, and all he could see in that unforgiving glass was fear.

Should he tell his wife? No! She would have nothing more to do with him. Would she throw him out? Yes! There would be no forgiveness. Confession may pacify the local priest but not her. Sooner or later, without friends or references, he would end up jobless, a down-and-out, a man of the road!

He lay on his bed and tried to think. He was not an evil man. He would go to the young couple and warn them that the bridge was not safe. Would they believe him? They would say that Jack was in league with the American. There seemed to be no way out when, out of sheer exhaustion, he fell asleep.

He awoke to find his wife shaking his shoulder, 'Wake up. You'll be late for work.'

Jack came out of his dreams into the nightmare of cruel reality where an unbelievable fact hung above his head like a precariously suspended sword. Had his mind become deranged? Had he, perhaps, had some kind of a seizure and imagined it all? No! The state of his clothes and the dirt on his face and hands were proof enough. He was scared . . .

He remembered the oxyacetylene equipment, that damning evidence, which had to be returned to the garage, and without bothering to wash or shave he ran downstairs, pushed past his wife, and disappeared out of the kitchen door. She crossed to the window in time to see Jack leave the tool shed with a large carrier bag. 'What do you think he's up to?' she asked the cat. 'Do you think he's had enough of us or something?'

Jack returned the oxyacetylene equipment to the garage. 'You took your time,' the mechanic complained. 'What have you been trying to do, break open a safe or something?'

'That drive shaft had really seized up and I had to be careful or I would have gone right through the metal!' There, he had said it! 'Cut through that and you could put your own life at risk, and anyone with you!'

Jack wanted to sit down. Did he know? How could he? Was this mechanic now trying to tell him that if anybody was killed he would be charged with murder?

'Hey, you look as if you've been overdoing it. I should have told you that burner was a bit of a blaster. Why don't you sit down and I'll get you some coffee.'

'No, I'm all right! Thanks.' Jack knew that if he drank a gallon of coffee his problem would still be there. He paid the man and, with a deep sinking feeling inside, went off in search of the monk. If anything went wrong, if the bridge did collapse, then at least he would have done everything possible to warn them.

He found Bill sitting alone in the little village park. He already looked quite depressed. 'Oh, it's you! You look as if the Missus has thrown you out and you've been sleeping rough!'

There is nothing like anger for bringing a man to his senses and Bill's remark was like a slap on the face.

'What's it to you. You're no more than a money-grabbing foreigner. You haven't got your own way yet!'

'I'm sure you will be delighted to know that we have been gazumped by some old American with pots of money.'

'Really?'

'Yes really, so if you have any inclination to

play trains I suggest you leave me alone and go and find Shute.'

Jack resisted the urge to make further comment and left as nonchalantly as he was able.

★ ★ ★

It did not take Jack long to track down the entrepreneurial American. 'Is it true that you are going into the railway business?'

'It is.' Shute confirmed, 'All we've got to do is get over that trial run tomorrow and it'll be a cinch!'

'Tomorrow?' Jack felt a knife twisting inside him.

'Yeah. I had a word with the old lady and everything's been fixed. We've been getting one of those old engines ready and we're going to pull some of that rolling stock.'

'That bridge is not safe!' Jack insisted.

Shute stood up. 'Not safe? Well now, how's that, when we've had the go-ahead from your very conscientious health and safely inspectors? What are you trying to do, put me off going through with this deal? I know you Welsh ain't very keen on outsiders.' He drew hard on his cigar and blew the smoke in Jack's general direction. 'I'm sure the locals who are looking for work will not feel the same way about it!'

'The bridge is not safe. When I went across it as a kid we could feel a definite movement. One of the local engineers took a look at it,' he lied, 'and he told me that one of the supports needed strengthening. If you take a train across, let alone any of those wagons, the whole thing might collapse!'

'Hey, come on! Who are you kidding?' Shute pulled his eyebrows together into deep frown. 'Ain't I seen you before somewhere?'

'Not to my knowledge.' Jack replied hesitatingly. He didn't like the look on this canny businessman's face one bit.

The American tossed his cigar butt into the gutter and laughed. 'I've got it. I've seen your face in the local paper. You're that Holy Jo. I thought it was the religious couple you had your knife in for bringing the village into disrepute. What's it to you what I do, anyway? We're taking that train across tomorrow and you can get lost!'

Shute strode away leaving Jack with the biggest problem of his life and nobody to share it with, except the police! And he tried not to think about that. The bridge was old. They built things well in those days. If that support did go would the other supports be enough to hold the rest of the structure up and prevent a disaster?

★　★　★

Jack wandered about for the rest of that day, scared to face his wife, and trying to work out a solution to what seemed to be an insoluble problem. In his mind he saw the flashing blue lights of the police car and he could hear that cold authoritative voice: 'Mr. Evans, we believe you can help us with our enquiries . . . '

He noticed that the local inn, The Shepherd's Inn, was open, and if ever he needed a good stiff drink it was right now!

The landlord knew Jack and like most landlords he welcomed a holy man turned sinner and, with a wink at his regular customers, he went to his assistance. 'What brings you in here?' Not getting any reply he tried again. 'What you can I get you?'

What should he choose? Should he play safe and stick to beer or wine, or go for one of the big exciting-looking bottles, which were ranged along a shelf behind the bar? 'Originally made by the monks of Loch Ailshe', the label on a twelve year old whisky said, and that had decided it.

'A large malt, please!'

The others, mostly working men, looked at him with a new interest. Everybody knew him, for hadn't they all read about him in the papers: a pious little man, who liked to interfere. Oh well, it was a good story and it made a change from all the other rather mundane stuff that was churned out in their pub. And here, in their very own bar, was this front-page character, this unholy bigot himself!

The malt whisky made him much happier and all those nagging worries about the bridge just seemed to fade away. Why, even if it did collapse, how could anybody possibly suspect him of having anything to do with it? After another drink he began to feel decidedly reckless, with a sudden urge to tell everybody how he had gone out there in the middle of the night with oxyacetylene equipment to sabotage the bridge. At that moment, he felt like a man at the edge of a precipice who has that wild abandon inside him, which says JUMP!

'I hear they are having a trial run on the old track tomorrow,' one of the men said.

If this bearer of local gossip had pointed a pistol at his head, Jack would not have been more startled. He struggled to regain his wits. 'As a matter of fact that bridge isn't safe. I did warn them, but the American wouldn't listen to me.'

'How do you know it isn't safe?'

'Eh?'

'How do . . . ' his interrogator was not going to be put off lightly.

'I travelled on it as a lad.' Jack answered hastily. 'It was dodgy then, and, to my knowledge, no repairs have been done since, so it stands to reason it must be dodgy now.'

Silently he congratulated himself for his ability to think on his feet, and considerably shocked by the realisation that he nearly opened his mouth and told all, Jack wondered how he could sober up quickly and not lose face. Food! A good meal was what he needed. His wife would have a good dinner waiting for him, but she was a bit too smart for his liking. Dare he take the risk that she would detect liquor on his breath or see a change in his demeanour? More time. He'd eat out. He couldn't remember the last time he'd had a meal in a restaurant, and he'd heard the Shepherd's Inn did home cooked local dishes . . .

'Landlord, can I see your menu?'

Jack was gratified to see a look on his host's face. His visit to the inn would be a source of gossip for a week or two, and no doubt his wife would get to hear about it. At that point in time he had far more pressing worries. Suppose they examined the bridge support and discovered those burn marks? Who would have an oxyacetylene burner? Why the local garage, of course! In his mind he could hear the police inspector, 'And would you be so kind as to show me the drive shaft, sir, the one which you said had seized up?'

He wondered what it was like to be shut up in prison. The barbaric conditions. Three men to a cell originally been built for one. Locked up for twenty-three hours out of twenty-four. The degrading business of slopping out. And what would happen to him when the other inmates discovered that he had been, of all things, a church warden?

If the bridge did collapse and there was injury or loss of life he could never bring himself to go to the police; the very thought of being shut up in a prison terrified him. He would say goodbye to his wife and make a run for it, find some place out in the wilds. Next minute these thoughts were dashed when he realised that he couldn't just run away and leave his family to face the music. Besides, the garage man would identify him, the police would hunt him down and he would be led away in handcuffs!

As he ate his excellent meal he thought about his life: past, present and future. How could he ever stand up and preach on the sins of others again . . .

★　★　★

Downhearted, Bill wandered around reflecting on his future, with or without Rosie. He passed the Friar's Table, and remembered the days before Toy, when a relaxed drink with friends in his local had been something to look forward to at the end of a hard working week.

If Bill thought his troubles were a private matter, he was much mistaken. By the silence that greeted him as he entered the bar, he suspected that he and Rosie were already the topic of conversation.

Unabashed the landlord asked him, 'What are you going to do if you can't buy the railway?'

It was kindly said and Bill could not take offence. 'Look around for some work, I suppose.'

'Could be difficult, you being a monk and all that,' he winked at his customers. 'Listen, we're short of staff, especially during the holidays. How about you helping us out during meal times?'

His wife jumped at the idea, 'A real monk here at the Friar's Table, my, that'd be a stunt!'

Bill wondered if they were serious or not. 'An ex-monk, now!' he corrected. 'Thank you for your offer; I will give it some thought.'

'Well, don't think too long. I've got an ad.

in for somebody this week.'

'Why don't you change the name and have done with it?' a customer suggested. 'Call it The Happy Monk!'

Bill realised he was enjoying himself. For the first time in ten years he could relax with a pint of beer and a few new friends.

12

For the second night running Jack came home to a silent house. The front door was unlocked and he went straight to bed, but again he couldn't sleep. All he could see was the train, packed with excitable passengers, coming up the long wooded incline towards that accursed bridge. If only he could have another drink. If only he could sink back into that same blissful state, which he had experienced at The Friar's Table! There was no drink in this house. He had never been allowed it!

The front door slammed and he sat up with a start. Was it the police already? He looked at his watch. Ten o'clock! He had been asleep when he should have been trying to find Shute. He hurried downstairs. The house was empty and there was a note from his wife: 'You came in late and I didn't want to disturb you. Nelly persuaded me to go into Pen to see the old train. It looks as if the whole village will be there. Could be fun. Come and join us.'

Jack was past caring who took over the railway. All his pent up hatred and feeling of revenge had gone. How could he get Shute to stop the train? He had never felt more alone.

He started off at a run, but it was a long way across the fields and when at last he came close to the town the train was already beginning to move out. It was Panting Bess and some old carriages . . . Jack breathed a sigh of relief; the trackside was packed with excitable people, but the carriages were empty. Newspaper reporters ran alongside the train with their photographers in tow. Jack gasped in horror. The nun was leaning out of the brake van! He heard her call out to the monk, 'The newspaper man wanted some photos of me in the train to show there is no hard feeling!' He had never trusted the press!

Jack, exhausted, struggled to get his breath. If he shouted out telling her to get her off the crowd would think he was crazy, and if anything did happen to the train they would believe that he was the number one suspect. He stood and stared at the billowing smoke, which screened the village boys running alongside the train, with their dogs. And then he ran, too. If he could catch up with the brake van on that long slow gradient through the woods, he could tell Rosie to jump. He tried to run, stumbling across the sleepers, but his previous night's visit to The Shepherd's Inn was taking its toll. The village youths, yelling wildly, were well up the hill; he just could not match their pace.

He could still see the train. Rosie was leaning out of the brake van. Jack shouted one last time. He knew it was in vain. There was no way she could hear him over the noise of the excited boys and the engine at that distance. And then the train driver, anxious to show off the mettle of his engine to the American buyer, increased his speed, and Jack watched it disappear from sight . . .

A loud bang made him jump. Then came a series of ear splitting thuds, the squeal of tortured metal and a hiss of steam. He heard the cries of panic-stricken people and he wanted to run . . . to be anywhere but here. The din from the bridge grew louder. How many had been killed? And Rosie? Had he killed her, too?

Men came running along the track towards him and their hot, angry faces seemed to say: 'You did it. You were responsible. You are the murderer!'

Jack put up his hands, but the monk pushed past him and ran on down the track yelling, 'Make way. It's the train. Get an ambulance . . . Get the police . . . Get the . . . '

Jack walked on towards the bridge. There, before his eyes, was the scene he had been planning: the derailed train and the carriages suspended over the bridge at crazy angles.

* * *

People were climbing down onto the track, and standing about in groups, talking excitedly. Regardless of his own safely, Bill scrambled down the embankment as fast as he could. 'Rosie, where is Rosie?'

Bewildered gazes met his enquiry, 'Who?'

'She was in the brake van.'

A young lad pointed, 'The nun's down there hanging over . . . '

The van, still connected to the rear carriage, had smashed through the parapet of the bridge and hung, suspended above the gorge like some grotesque pendulum.

'Rosie!'

Bill started to climb down, only to be grabbed by a swarthy onlooker. 'Are you mad? Look at the coupling, it's practically sheared through.'

'I don't care. I must get to her.'

'Don't be a fool man. Any extra weight on the van will finish it off, and you'll kill her.'

The screech of metal as the seesaw motion of the brake van cut into the coupling was warning enough of Rosie's peril. 'The other couplings are OK, I can go down through the carriages . . . ' Bill climbed up on to the parapet of the bridge, moving as quickly as he could to the last carriage. Inside he climbed down, across the seating until he reached the rear door. It was already hanging open. Thankfully Bill saw the brake van just beneath him, swinging menacingly. An arid whiff of smoke from the overheated coupling made him choke. He glanced at the two-hundred-foot drop, and his blood turned ice cold.

Rhythmic shrieks from the tortured metal penetrated his fear. 'Rosie!'

'Oh, Bill, be careful.'

The coupling was greasy, why hadn't he expected that! His grip tightened as he worked his way down, inch by inch, until he stood on the brake van. Oil dripped down from the carriage above, every step had to be tested. At last he reached the door to the guard's compartment-jammed! In tears, Bill struggled in vain to open it. Had he come so far only for them both to fall to their deaths?

A yell from above. He looked up to see a something snaking down. It would be a hell of a risk to take, but Bill fell onto the rope, and, as if in one movement, bent his knees and let himself fall against the side. Straightening his legs he propelled himself into the air, and with all the force he could muster smashed the door open with his heels.

He found Rosie lying on the partition, now the floor, terrified, shaking. Bill had never seen her like this — so vulnerable — too scared to move, even to save herself.

'Rosie, come, take my arm.' Bill wanted so much to go to her and gather her up in his arms, but this was no time for soft words, he must take command and overcome her fear. 'Quick, Rosie, you must do as I say.'

She opened her eyes. Encouraged by Bill's determined expression she proffered her hand. 'Bill, I am so scared.'

'I know you are, Rosie, reach out as far as you can.'

Bill trod gingerly on the van, it lurched suddenly. He had no choice. He reached in and unceremoniously grabbed her. Fastening the rope round her he balanced on the platform and signalled for the men to pull her up. His eyes followed her ascent until shearing metal cried out a warning to him. Desperately, he climbed back up through the carriage to the bridge.

Brother Bill was a hero; he was carried on the shoulders of young men to the ambulance where Rosie lay waiting for him.

'Nothing to worry about,' the paramedic assured him. 'Only bruises. Your Rosie's had a bit of a battering, but no real damage done.'

'Rosie . . . '

Rosie laughed at his tear stained face and held out her hand to him, 'Oh, Bill, what will I do without you?'

★   ★   ★

The press had taken their pictures and even the local television company had rushed reporters to the scene. For hadn't this reverend monk rescued the nun, Sister Mary Rose, from certain death? Bill found himself wondering about that small stepping stone, which lay, so slippery and insecure, between life and death. If Rosie had died his world would have been shattered. As it was, nobody had been hurt and, with the help of a skilful crane driver the brake van had been rescued. But once again he and Rosie were headline news!

The next day Bill and Rosie came face to face with a red-faced Shute. 'I'll tell you what I think of your railways. I thought you British could build bridges. First time I cross one a train is derailed. Why, that whole railroad system is not fit for a museum!'

'Does that mean you're not going to buy it after all?' Bill asked.

'You're too darn right, I'm not. I could have taken a dive right into that gorge. Next

200

thing, the tunnel'll fall in on me or the darned engine'll blow up!'

Instead of going home, Bill and Rosie took the road that led them up to Mrs. Thomas's nursing home. The old lady had heard about the accident and wanted all the detail. 'You are far too modest,' she told Bill 'I am sure it was a lot more dangerous than you say!'

Eventually, they were able to steer the conversation away from the recent dramas to the sale. 'The reason we came is that we understand Mr. Shute is no longer interested in the railway,' Rosie explained.

The old lady smiled, 'I always wanted you two to have it. I have some good news! The bridge, in fact the whole railway, is insured. The premium, in those days, was small. A railway system, including bridges and tunnels, was reckoned to be virtually indestructible.'

'The bridge can be repaired at no charge to you at all?' Bill asked her.

'Yes, because there has been an accident. The insurance company will come out and make the usual investigation, of course, and arrange all the necessary repairs. You won't even have to pay for any more reports. They will do everything.'

★ ★ ★

Jack heard on the grapevine that the monk and his nun were definitely buying the narrow gauge railway, and since the 'accident' had occurred before the purchase, the old lady's insurance company had been called in. Anxious days followed sleepless nights; all he could do was to think about the consequences of his actions. How thorough would the inspectors be? Would the sabotage be found?

His mind was in a whirl; the garage man was pointing at him and he could see the flashing blue lights of the police car. If anybody had been killed he would have got life. Sabotaging a bridge with intent to wreck a train? He would probably get life anyway!

One afternoon, when his wife had gone into Pen to do some shopping, he rummaged around in his garage. Surely in the many tins of paint there would be one of right colour. As far as he could remember the bridge was a dirty grey colour. There! Just what he needed. He picked up an old paintbrush and stood it on the tin in readiness. If he could just touch up those burn marks and then get back under cover of dark . . .

He put the paint into a plastic bag and set off across the fields in the direction of the bridge. It was eerily quiet. When he came to the bridge he was careful to stay out of sight until he was sure nobody was about. He examined his earlier handiwork and was glad that he had come: anybody could see that the support had sunk almost a foot. The bridge was a murky green, not grey at all. Still better to go ahead and paint the support, try and disguise the damage as best he could, he thought.

Blast! How could he open the tin with his bare hands? He found a piece of flint to lever off the lid. The sun was already low when he went to work, all the time scared that somebody, even the American, might come out there. A loud fluttering noise set his heart racing, he gasped and he looked up to see who his discoverer could be — to see a flock of pigeons coming into roost. Unnerved he wanted to drop everything and run. He steeled himself to stay and see the task through; his very liberty depended on it.

Finished at last, he stood back to see the effect from a distance. His heart sank. The support with its shiny new paint looked more damning than ever. The ground was hard and stony; he chipped at it with the flint and scooped some dirt up in his hands and threw it at the wet paint, repeating the process until the camouflage was complete. For good measure, he stacked some big stones round the base of the support until the grey paint, and all his mischief, was hidden. All he could do now was to hope that the insurance inspector would not be too thorough.

It was dark when he had finished. With no moon to light his way, he had no choice but to follow the railway line back across the wooded countryside to Pen. He breathed a sigh of relief as the last bus of the night to Treriver came into sight.

The front door was unlocked. His wife had long since gone to bed.

Slowly and carefully he climbed into bed next to her and settled down for the first peaceful sleep for days. He lay back and mused on the evening's events; quietly congratulating himself for his intelligence and cunning. It was such a shame that he would never be able to tell anyone about his brilliance. It would have to be his personal secret. And with a self satisfied grin on his face he drifted off to sleep.

But not for long — within the hour he sat bolt upright. 'Oh, no! Stupid, bloody fool!' he shouted.

He bit his bottom lip, as inevitably his wife was aroused from her slumbers. 'What? Did you say something, Jack?'

He patted her on the head as he might a little child, 'Nothing to worry about, my love, you go back to sleep. I just had a bit of a nightmare, that's all.' Not in the least convinced she obeyed. She would deal with her husband in her own time and her own way . . .

Nightmare! Jack wished it were. This was stark reality! He had been so pleased with his efforts to cover all traces of his crime, and in so much haste to get away in the darkness, that he had left the paintbrush and the partly used tin of paint back at the bridge!

★ ★ ★

Jack's wife was worried. He had been coming in late, not eating properly, and she'd found him missing from the marital bed on more than one occasion . . .

Almost silently, the front door was being closed . . . He was off on one of his mysterious errands again! She grabbed her coat from the hallstand and violently flung open the door, determined to run after him and demand an explanation. But the road leading down to the village was empty. Puzzled she looked around. There he was, making his way across the field to the woods. What on earth was he up to? There was nothing up there, except the railway, and the train had been put back on the rails and taken back to Pen . . . He hadn't even bothered to have his breakfast or speak to her first . . . Was he avoiding her?

Her fragmented thoughts began to come together, and like a jigsaw the more pieces that fitted the clearer became the picture! She had been aware for sometime that any mention of the railway, any titbit of gossip he overheard her sharing with neighbours had riled him . . . 'No wonder!' she spat out through her teeth. 'The blighter has been meeting someone up there, in the old sheds! I bet they never thought anyone would discover their love nest out in the wilds . . . '

Her forehead tensed into a deep frown. She mustn't be hasty. She needed to think it through for a second or two . . .

It was a lovely day. It was going to be hot. What could be more natural than to go for a nice walk in the early sunshine. She would follow him.

But when she started to cross the field she lost sight of him. Convinced the railway held the key to her enigma, she climbed up into the wood until she reached the track. She paused for breath, and to think about the best way to reach the sheds. 'I don't fancy crossing that bridge, but I'm not going to go down into the gorge and up again . . . '

★   ★   ★

Whereas his wife had no inclination to descend the depths of the gorge, making sure he wasn't being watched, Jack made haste to climb down the embankment to the foot of the bridge. With relief he saw his paintbrush and the tin of paint. He stood back and looked at his efforts to hide his crime with appreciation. The heavy stones might have been put there by a gang of railway workers. It was surprising how much strength a man can muster when his adrenalin is running! He threw the brush into a crevice in the rocks below him and tossed the tin of paint in after it, and then he heard it . . . A laugh! But the voice was clearly not amused . . .

Jack looked up. Standing akimbo, there was his wife! 'What on earth are you doing, casting out devils?'

Jack, scared that she might have seen the tin of paint, and lost for words forced a smile. 'You could say that!'

He climbed back up the embankment. 'I was throwing some stones in among the rocks down there. When I was a kid I used to make them spin!'

'What on earth made you come all the way out here?'

'Oh, I haven't been able to sleep for nights thinking about that bridge and what could have caused the accident, so I thought I'd come out and have a look round myself.'

'Did you find anything?'

'No, but somebody seems to have had a go at strengthening it before. Look at all those big stones down there. Some poor chap has been sweating out his guts!'

'You said chap . . . why would you think one man did it? Surely a gang of blokes would be put on a job like that?' She got no reply. 'And why is it any particular concern of yours?'

'Eh?'

'And why come down here at the crack of dawn? It's unlike you to miss your breakfast . . . '

If he knew his canny wife, he was going to have to come up with a very good explanation for his bizarre behaviour. He needed time to think. 'Let's go home. I'm starving. I'll tell you while we eat.'

13

The insurance company carried out a thorough inspection of the bridge and the repairs associated with the accident were agreed with all parties.

'There are other places where rust is starting to set in. These sections didn't have any bearing on the accident, but they will need to be added to your maintenance schedule for attention within the next few years. And some cowboys have left some cutting unfinished. They even had the cheek to pile some rocks up to hide it! It was them that caught our eye. It has certainly weakened that leg and should be seen to as soon as possible. Nothing a competent welder cannot put right.'

'That's wonderful!' Bill and Rosie left the insurance agent's arm in arm, relieved and very happy.

But their elation did not last long. Rosie tugged Bill's sleeve. He put his head down to hear what she was trying to whisper in his ear. Given her excited mood, he expected to hear some endearment or word of encouragement, instead he thought he heard her say, 'It's the Reverend Mother!'

He smiled and looked into her face, more than willing to act as a stooge for her jesting . . . but her expression told him that this was no joke. He looked up to see an elderly, serious-faced nun bearing down on them. It was the dreaded cleric he had heard so much about, and by the way she was advancing upon Rosie she had not arrived in Wales to invite her out to tea! 'Steady on, old girl. We'll see this thing through together!'

★ ★ ★

In her younger days, the Reverend Mother had often thought about what life would be like outside the Abbey. But she had long ceased to have any doubts. She had lived at St. John's for over forty years, and truly believed that a life of prayer in a closed order was the best way to serve her fellow man and get closer to God.

As usual she was scanning one of the daily newspapers to find subjects for prayer when she spotted the headline: 'Monk rescues nun from doomed guard's van!' 'It can't be . . . Not again!' But she knew even before she read the article that it would be about Sister Mary Rose.

There lying on the heavy oak desk were pictures of a young woman being lifted out of a derailed train. This was the end! Sister Mary Rose, already absent without leave, and in disgrace for running off with a so-called monk, had got herself into the papers yet again.

The Mother Superior with the excuse that she was responsible for the welfare of her nuns, both in this life and in the next, gained approval from the Bishop to set forth in search of her lost sheep. She came face to face with Bill and Rosie in their village High Street and, though she had not seen Rosie in civilian clothes since she had entered the convent, recognised her immediately and quickly crossed herself.

The Reverend Mother had already decided it would be best to be friendly and, without looking at Bill, made an attempt to smile. An expression that may have disturbed her lips, but did not reach her eyes. 'I came to see if you were all right, my dear. You have been away from us for such a long time. I wanted to tell you that if your mother's affairs have now been wound up we should both go home together . . . '

★ ★ ★

Home! How could the convent with its dark and draughty corridors, be called home? It was more like an asylum. Home! She remembered the happy place, the loving people she had left behind all those years ago. True, they loved you at the convent, but it was a rather austere sort of love and not at all like the affection which her parents had bestowed upon her.

Rosie held on to Bill's sleeve. The writers of the psalms, all the great philosophers of mankind, had directed their thoughts towards the outside world. And this was what Rosie had wanted to do. This was what she had tried to see from her cell window. This was the land of her dreams. In that moment, as she clutched at Bill for support, these thoughts were instinctive, her only defence, as she prepared to answer the woman who was God's representative at St. John's Abbey.

Maybe if she had thought about it all more thoroughly, if she had worked things out for herself, she could have left the convent years ago, while she was still young. She began to wonder whether putting things out of your mind, crushing them automatically before they stood a chance of making any sense, was irresponsible, and therefore sinful. Had she, then, by staying on, become a sinner? Her mind in such a muddle . . .

No, when she remembered her vows she knew there was no alternative but to stick it out. She had promised to accept discomfort and unhappiness, gladly, for Christ, and she knew she would have to go back to the convent with the Reverend Mother.

Rosie tried to explain that she had been delayed over her mother's affairs, but the Reverend Mother took her by the arm and, talking earnestly to her, escorted her back along the street to the small hotel where she was staying.

★ ★ ★

Bill was uneasy. Reverend Mother would very soon learn about Rosie's proposed purchase of the railway and she would remind her that it was a violation of her vows; that no nun was allowed to purchase anything, let alone property. She would take Rosie back with her before she could sign the papers!

The Reverend Mother would see it as her responsibility to save her sinning nun at all costs; it was the very essence of her beliefs. How could he send her back on the train without the woman he loved, and wanted to marry?

He would have a quiet word with the Reverend Mother and settle the matter once and for all. He was not yet sure what he was going to say, but somehow he would persuade her that she had made a wasted journey and that she would have to return to the convent alone! Bill swallowed hard. After all marriage was a holy estate!

Bill was devastated when he learned the Reverend Mother had persuaded Rosie to honour her vows and return to the convent the very next day. Moved to desperation, he found out where the Reverend Mother was staying, called on her and went straight to the point. 'Sister Mary Rose and I would like to be partners and run the business together, and, if she can get a dispensation from the Vatican to be released from her vows, we would like to be married!'

'You talk about getting a dispensation from the Vatican as if you were buying a box of chocolates! Sister Mary Rose's vows can never be broken and, if by associating herself with you she has committed a sin, she will have the rest of her life in St. John's Abbey to look for atonement.' The Reverend Mother held the large wooden crucifix, which hung from a chain around her neck, up to his face. 'As for marriage, she is married already — to God!'

Bill had nothing to lose and played his last card. 'Sister Mary Rose and I have been living together since we met in Yugoslavia.'

That sounded awful and he knew it, but if he thought it would shake the Reverend Mother he was mistaken. 'I have dealt with countless sinners in my time, not the least of which has been one of my own nuns; I have long become inured to the common fact of unmarried couples living together. If anything this strengthens my resolve to take Rosie back.' Bill pleaded, 'Look, Sister Mary Rose and I would be very happy together. We could run this railway and go to church and live good Christian lives. Sister Mary Rose has too much going for her to throw it all away for the rest of her life. I am quite sure that both God and Sister Mary Rose would be much happier if you could let her go!'

'I have read about you in the newspapers,' the Reverend Mother pointed to her newspaper. 'You were expelled from St. Joseph's, because you tried to take Sister Mary Rose into the monastery with you. You say you want to marry her, but I believe you just want to use her and her money to get the railway for yourself.'

Bill could have struck the woman. Somehow, he had to get Rosie away from her, but he knew that it would be easier to knock down her Abbey with a shovel than to get this woman to see his point of view. His only chance was to get Rosie to change her mind, but he hadn't seen her all day. 'Where is Sister Mary Rose? What have you done with her?'

'What do you mean, what have I done with her? Do you think I have chained her up, hand and foot, or something? She is staying here at the hotel with me and we are going back to St. John's on the first train tomorrow morning!'

Bill began to feel an even deeper despair. Everything he had wanted, all the happiness he had dreamed about, had come to nothing! 'But there are papers to be signed, affairs to be tied up in connection with the railway!'

'Then I am afraid it will all have to be undone and Mrs. Thomas will have to sell the railway to somebody else!'

Bill knew he was beaten. The Reverend Mother would join the ranks of the martyrs rather than give an inch. He left the room without another word.

At the reception desk he enquired after Rosie, 'She's in room 108 . . . ' and to the astonishment of the desk clerk, Bill took the stairs two at a time to the first floor. There was a long pause before she came to the door. She opened it cautiously, 'Bill!' and looked up and down the corridor anxiously.

'Don't worry, she is still downstairs. I have

just been to see her. Oh Rosie, is it all going to end, all our hopes and dreams?'

'I have taken my vows, Bill,' she said miserably, 'and I suppose the Reverend Mother is right and I should see it all through. I wanted to leave you enough money to buy the railway, but she says that I should give it all to St. John's and, because she is God's representative at the Abbey I should obey her wishes.'

'No, Rosie, I love you and I will not let you go . . . ' Bill exclaimed bitterly.

'I am sorry, Bill, but I must go back.'

He wanted to tell her she was talking rubbish, but he knew he would be wasting his time. Maybe he should return to the monastery and plead for forgiveness and re-entry. Maybe, behind those great walls, he would have something in common with Rosie and he would feel a little closer to her . . .

'Please don't come and see me off at the station tomorrow,' she added, 'let's say goodbye now!'

Bill couldn't believe it. Rosie might just as well have told him she was going to die. He couldn't believe that this was goodbye forever.

'Change your mind, Rosie. This is where it all happens, here in the outside world. This is the place where dreams are made, not shut up in a gloomy old convent!'

She smiled and shook her head.

Bill tried to swallow and the words seemed to stick in his throat. 'Is it really goodbye, after all we've been through?'

She nodded, her eyes wet, and as she turned to go Bill put his arms round her and kissed her. 'That kiss will have to last me a lifetime.'

★ ★ ★

Bill decided he would go to the railway station. He longed to see Rosie, even if it were for the last time. Thorndyke said he would go, too.

A small crowd of villagers had gathered at the station, and one or two newspaper reporters, anxious to get another picture of Rosie, waited there with their photographers. Father Connolly and the Reverend Mother stood talking together on the platform. Rosie was there, standing on her own, dressed in her nun's ankle length gown. The train was just coming in as Bill reached the platform. The Reverend Mother gave him a penetrating look, hustled Rosie into the carriage and climbed in after her.

Bill didn't like goodbyes. He hadn't said goodbye to anyone of importance in his life since Sarah had slipped away from him all those years ago. And here Rosie was being taken away . . .

A shrill whistle warned of the train's imminent departure. Bill tried to find the right words, but could only choke on his tears. 'Rosie . . . '

The train slowly pulled away leaving him frozen to the spot. Thorndyke came and stood beside him, 'I'm so sorry, Bill. I can't believe she has actually gone back.'

'What am I going to do without her?' Tears fell unashamedly down his weather-beaten cheeks.

'I don't know, mate. I really don't know.' Thorndyke wished there were something he could say to make things easier for his grieving friend. It wasn't often he was lost for words. 'Come on, let's go back home . . . '

★ ★ ★

Rosie's cottage seemed cold and empty without her. The two men sat down on hard wooden chairs and faced each other across the kitchen table. Neither wanted the comfort of the little sitting room. 'You know what we need?' Thorndyke asked. 'A stiff drink!'

'I can't see how getting drunk is going to do any good. It won't bring her back.'

'You please yourself. But I'm going to find the whisky.'

'You do what you like. I'm going to . . . '

Thorndyke never found out what Bill had in mind. 'Can't you hear the door bell ringing?'

Bill put his head in his hands, 'You answer it.'

'But I'm looking for the booze.'

'Don't answer it then. I don't care!'

'All right! I'll go. It will be the solicitor again, I expect. As if we can sort out this unholy mess,' Thorndyke muttered to himself as he went.

★   ★   ★

Bill got up and wandered out into the back garden, anywhere away from the front of the house. He wasn't prepared to talk to any visitors. He just wanted to wallow in his depression. In a funny kind of way he found comfort in it.

The flowers were so beautiful they couldn't fail to lift his mood. He smiled. In his mind's eye he could see her — standing at the back door. He looked down, not knowing if he wanted the haunting image to stay with him forever or to go and leave him in peace. She was telling him off as she had done so many times, 'You've got a touch of the poor-me's, Bill.' Tears stung his eyes again. 'Nothing a walk in the hills won't cure.' Was he going mad? He turned to go in, keeping his eyes to the ground so Thorndyke would not see his tears. He put his hand up to push the door open.

'That's a fine welcome, I must say!'

He opened his eyes wide. There on the doorstep was a pair of sensible black shoes, half hidden by the skirt of a black gown . . . 'Rosie?' Dare he hope? He blinked. Again. Gathering her up into his arms he swept her inside. Neither knew whether to laugh or cry. Covering her upturned face with kisses, through tears now of happiness, he declared, 'Rosie, I love you.'

'I know, Bill.'

With her still in his arms he said, 'Sister Mary Rose, will you do me the honour of becoming my wife?'

'Yes, Bill, I will, because I love you with all my heart.'

★　★　★

Thorndyke brought the lovers back to reality. 'I think it is time for me to make a hasty exit. Don't want to be a gooseberry and all that! And I need a drink. But before I go, I've just got to know how you got away! What made you change your mind?'

'It was when the train went into a long tunnel. I just knew that I couldn't go back to the enclosed life of the Abbey, and leave the only man I have ever truly loved. And I also knew that, wherever we are, God would love me, and Bill,' she laughed, 'and even you, Thorndyke!'

She kissed Bill on the cheek, 'It was easy. I just told the Reverend Mother, 'If I return to the Abbey I shall be living a lie.' And she gave me a blessing, and the money for the return trip, and told me to get out at the next station.'

'I can see that I shall have to find some other lodgings. Leave you two love-birds on your own.' Thorndyke teased.

'Don't you even think about it, you are family, now.' Bill laughed. 'And we shall need a chaperone until we are married, or we really shall be the talk of the village.'

★   ★   ★

The wedding was supposed to be a simple affair. But the villagers had other ideas. Everyone was happy to celebrate the union of this unusual couple. The whole village was better off for their coming. The publicity had certainly increased the visitor numbers and work in the area, for which many were grateful.

Jack's wife had completed the picture of her metaphorical jigsaw puzzle. Since no harm was done, she would not go so far as to report her husband's crime.

'I'm so glad Mrs. Thomas can look out of her window and watch the trippers enjoying the train ride, and the views across the valley,' Rosie mused.

'I know.' Bill hugged her tightly, 'No regrets?'

'No, none.' She cocked her head onto one side and added thoughtfully, 'I wonder what the Reverend Mother is doing now!'

Bill grinned. 'Maybe she is lighting a candle for Rosie!'

'What a nice idea. Let's go down to the village and light one for her.'

We do hope that you have enjoyed reading this large print book.

Did you know that all of our titles are available for purchase?

We publish a wide range of high quality large print books including:
Romances, Mysteries, Classics
General Fiction
Non Fiction and Westerns

Special interest titles available in large print are:
The Little Oxford Dictionary
Music Book
Song Book
Hymn Book
Service Book

Also available from us courtesy of Oxford University Press:
Young Readers' Dictionary
(large print edition)
Young Readers' Thesaurus
(large print edition)

For further information or a free brochure, please contact us at:
Ulverscroft Large Print Books Ltd.,
The Green, Bradgate Road, Anstey,
Leicester, LE7 7FU, England.
Tel: (00 44) 0116 236 4325
Fax: (00 44) 0116 234 0205

Other titles published by
The House of Ulverscroft:

THIRTEEN

Sebastian Beaumont

Stephen Bardot, a taxi driver working the exhausting night shift in Brighton, begins to experience alterations to his perception of reality . . . He regularly takes Valerie from 13 Wish Road to the Cornerstone Community Centre. She is terminally ill, so when he is no longer asked to collect her, he fears that she is dead. Making enquiries about her he discovers that her address does not exist — there is no number thirteen at Wish Road. Life gets weirder and he must walk away from the twilight world of Thirteen. But Thirteen has no intention of letting him go . . .

BED REST

Sarah Bilston

Quinn 'Q' Boothroyd is a busy, successful young English lawyer, married to the gorgeous Tom and living in New York. But when her doctor tells her she has to spend the last three months of her pregnancy on bed rest, Quinn is thrown into a tailspin by the idea of losing her social and professional life. Initially bored and frustrated, Quinn gradually finds herself re-examining her world — her marriage, relationships with family and friends, and her job. Indeed, bed rest produces some very surprising, funny and touching results . . .